D1544844

The Queen's Brooch

Marcus, son of a Roman Tribune, is brought to Britain at the age of seven. He grows up with the Celts, learning their languages and dialects, their customs and superstitions. When Marcus is in his teens he is named a tribune. He is reluctant, but accepts the appointment and is schooled to be a warrior. In a series of conflicts, Marcus fights Queen Boadicea's men, and later becomes one of her chieftains. He witnesses great battles and barbaric slaughter on both sides, and sees most of his friends die. In the end he comes to the conclusion that he must decide his own future course and has the courage to face the consequences of his decision.

the queen's BROOch

HENRY TREECE

G. P. Putnam's Sons

New

York

Published simultaneously in the Dominion of Canada by Longmans Canada Limited, Toronto

Library of Congress Catalog Card Number: 67–24177

Printed in the United States of America
12214

Contents

I

The Brooch

WHEN MARCUS VOLUSENUS was a boy of seven his father Ostorius, a very grand tribune of the ninth legion stationed at Lindum, sent home to Carthago Novo in Spain for the boy to come to him in Britain. In his letter to the boy's stepmother he made the garrison scribe write: "All is well here, and my son will be safe. The madman Caratacus has now been driven into the western mountains and will give us no more trouble. Do not delay in sending Marcus to me, my dear wife, for this humid climate may cure his cough where the physicians fail to do so. I have always been convinced that this cough is due rather to the summer dust of our country than to any weakness in the boy's constitution. In any event, he will be better under my eye, among the soldiers here, than wasting his time on the shore with the Africans who, as you told me in your last letter, are flooding into our city. In Britain the people are much as we Romans were earlier in our history. Marcus will learn from them certain manly virtues which might not be seen in Rome itself today. Of course, his accent will grow worse, for these Britons have a language of their own and make little effort to pronounce ours correctly; but, all told, the boy will benefit. I would rather have a son who spoke roughly but was a man, than one who spoke prettily but ran away when he saw a sword come out. Tell our daughter, Livia, that the next ship will carry a doll for her, dressed in the Celtic fashion with colored clothes and a bronze necklet. Tell her that it will have yellow hair, but that this is how the people look here. She will not believe it, but she must learn the truth some day. I expect you are well. You always are. Farewell. Ostorius."

For a month or two little Marcus Volusenus was unhappy in the great echoing stone garrison at Lindum. He missed his sister and his dog and the sea, and the household Africans who carried him on their shoulders into the swishing waves. Instead, he watched the soldiers drilling many hours every day, went to school with ten British boys who wore their flaxen hair onto their shoulders and had to learn everything by memory, because no one seemed to write anything down in Britain.

Then his father bought him a white pony and the world changed overnight. He forgot Carthago Novo and the Africans. He only dreamed of his dog and sister once a month now. And because all the grooms at Lindum were British, he had to learn Celtic. He was amazed how easy it was. Once Tigidius, one of the most important centurions, spoke to him on the edge of the parade ground and said, "Why Marcus, when you came here you spoke Latin like a true Spaniard. But now you babble at it like a duck. You are a credit to your British teacher, my boy."

Marcus told his father proudly what the great man had said. His father paced up and down the room awhile, then said, "Very well, we will see who gabbles like a duck. He shall have seven extra guard duties for that."

Marcus thought that this was a great honor for the centurion. But when he met the man next time all he got in return for his smile was a black-browed frown.

Still, he had the white horse. And when his father had his next leave from the legion, they rode down past the green marshes to see the city of Venta Icenorum, one of the great tribal capitals.

Marcus was very disappointed. It was only a lot of thatched huts, set at all angles, with little vegetable gardens surrounded by low, dry-stone walls. There were no pretty cypresses and no fountains. But there were lots of pigs grunting among the hawthorns, and big midden heaps at every crossroad that were always covered with swarms of flies.

Marcus didn't mind the flies too much but his white pony did and shied when they came buzzing about his head.

They stayed at the villa of another tribune who had left the legion to cultivate vines in that part. His name was Gaius Domitius and he had a stiff leg that he had got when a chariot ran over him at Camulodunum. He always stumped about leaning on a thick blackthorn stick and striking terror into the hearts of his forty British slaves. Marcus thought that Gaius Domitius must be very like the god Mithras, but his father looked stern when the boy told him this. He said, "Marcus, my son, I will tolerate almost any kind of stupidity in one of your age, but now you must learn once and for all that one does not compare the god with any man, however strong that man. The god is the god, and not to be compared."

Marcus said, "Our grooms at Lindum do not say Mithras. They say Mabon, and sometimes Belatucader. Can I compare these gods with men, then?"

His father shook his head and said, "Certainly not, boy. It is all the same thing. We call him Mithras. They call him something else. That is their affair, not ours. But we must behave like gentlemen and must give the god his proper respect, whatever his local name may be. Gaius Domitius is a man; a very fine man, naturally, being a Roman, but a man. Mithras is a god. Is that clear?"

Marcus said that it was, but it wasn't. He still thought that Mithras must be very like Gaius Domitius; but now

9

he had sense enough not to say everything he thought out loud.

Then while they were still in Icenian territory, a strange thing happened. A horse-slave, named Rudda called for Marcus one morning and offered to take him out riding to a place where there were some ancient stones. It was midday when they reached the place, which was all overgrown with nettles and willow herb, with the stones standing up in a crazy circle among the weeds. Many of them were chipped at the edges and most of them blackened with fire. Rudda pointed to them so that Marcus should see them, but he would not go near them himself. In fact, he would not look at them directly, but held one hand over his eyes like a shade if there was any danger of seeing them.

Marcus said, "What do you call them, Rudda?"

But the slave shook his head and said, "They have a name but I must not say it. If I said it, a bad thing would happen to me."

Marcus said, "You Britons are very funny, aren't you? You do not laugh as much as the Africans, but you are much funnier."

The slave said, "If you please to think so, sir."

Marcus said, "There you are again, calling me 'sir'. I am only a boy. You are twice as old as I am. You would call Gaius Domitius 'sir', or my father. But not me. Why do you do these funny things?"

Rudda said, "We do not think they are funny. They are our customs."

Marcus said, "Well, I still say they are funny, call them customs if you please. Come on, let's gallop down that sunken road. It looks so strange and mysterious with the oak branches leaning low over it."

But the slave shook his head and said, "No, no, sir! That road is forbidden. I am not allowed to set foot on it."

Marcus turned in his saddle and said, "Forbidden? By whom is it forbidden? It looks open enough to me. There is no chain across it to stop anyone. How is it forbidden, you funny fellow?"

Rudda clasped his hands and said, "It is the sacred road that leads to the stones. If I were to tread on it, a bad thing would happen to me."

Then Marcus lost all patience and said, "Well, you can please yourself, with these bad things that are always going to happen to you, but I like the look of that road and I am going to ride along it to see what is around the corner at the top of the hill. You can cut across the moorland and find me farther on, if you choose. But I am going."

So he swung his white pony around and dug his heels in the beast's sides and was soon away like the wind. The road was really little more than a mud track, baked hard by the sun, and flanked on either side by tall elders and wild briars, with oak trees above them and, here and there, a flowering thorn. It was exciting to ride this track because suddenly it fell into a steep hollow where the shadows from the trees almost blotted out the sunlight. A hare loped across the road in front of the white pony, and for a moment Marcus was almost thrown. But then the track climbed upward again before it disappeared around a high bank of ferns.

Marcus put the white pony at this slope gaily, shouting encouragement as he drummed with his heels. Then just when he was at the top and swinging round the ferns, his heart almost jumped into his mouth.

Coming toward him and filling the track were horsemen on shaggy ponies and carrying tall lances. They wore wolfskins about their shoulders and great iron helmets with bulls' horns at the sides, which made them look very fierce indeed. But it was the woman who rode before them all on a black horse that most startled Marcus, for he had never seen anyone like her in his life. She was dressed like a man, with a wolfskin jacket and hide-breeches bound round with colored thongs of braid. Her helmet hung on the saddle-horn and her thick hair flowed onto her shoulders, as russet as a fox's pelt. Marcus noticed all the gold rings and bronze bracelets she wore, but what caught his eye most of all was the strange tattoo-mark in blue in the middle of her forehead. It was in the form of a watching eye. And on her cheeks were other streaks of blue, in lines, that gave her a very savage look.

At first he thought she was going to ride him down, for she made no effort to pull in her black horse. But just at the last moment, when he was wondering what on earth he should do, she stopped and stared at him silently, her eyes wide open and angry. This made him feel very young and very helpless; but he remembered that his father was a tribune and so he sat there in the middle of the track and tried to put on the expression of *dignitas*.

After a very long time the woman leaned a little to one side of her horse's tall neck and said to him in very fair Latin, "I think you must be ten."

Marcus smiled, although the woman was not smiling, and said, "No, I am eight. But I am big for my age."

The woman said, "When you speak to me you must say 'My lady.' "

Marcus tried to frown at this, but in the end he said, "Very well, my lady."

Then the woman nodded and said, "That is your first lesson in manners, Roman. Now, since you are eight years old, you should know enough to declare your own name properly."

This time Marcus felt very stubborn. He said, "I am not used to telling my name to every stranger I meet on the road, *my lady*." He said the last two words very loudly so that she would see the sort of people Romans were. But she did not seem to care and said, "I am not a stranger, but you are. This is not your road, but it is mine. There are certain words I could say to the warlords who ride with me, and then you would be in a very awkward position indeed. Yes, very awkward. So have the goodness to state your name, aged eight."

So Marcus, very crest-fallen, gave his name and said who his father was and with whom they were staying. And when he had finished, the woman beckoned him to come closer to her. And when he sat almost beneath her shadow, she said, "I am the queen here. Can you understand that?"

Marcus nodded, feeling most ashamed now. The woman said, "My name is Boadicea, which in your language means the Victorious One."

She waited awhile, and to fill in the silence, Marcus said, "Then, my lady, I am sorry that I galloped along your road. I thought that it looked exciting. That is all."

The queen stared at him for a while with a frown on her forehead. Then she said strangely, "Yes, it is exciting to many who go down it. It is so exciting that they wish they might never come to the end of it, but that they could fly away like birds straightway."

Then for the first time Marcus noticed there was a man on foot at the end of the column of horsemen. His wrists were tied and he had a wound on one side of his head. It was unbandaged and the flies were troubling the man, but the horsemen didn't seem to mind.

Marcus said, "What has that poor man done, my lady? He looks very sad."

For a moment Queen Boadicea frowned again, this time quite angrily. But then she shook her head and smiled. "I do not ask you about your private affairs, do I?" she said. "I do not ask you who showed you this road, do I?"

Marcus said stoutly, "If you did I shouldn't tell you."

Then at the last moment he remembered to say, "My lady."

Suddenly the queen seemed to lose all interest in him. She called out to the warlords in a harsh language and they prepared to ride on. Then she looked down at Marcus again and felt in the deerskin pouch at her side. In her hand she held a round bronze brooch, on which was moulded a shape like a stag leaping, but all done in strips of metal joined together so that, unless you looked very carefully, you could not tell what it represented.

She held this brooch out to the boy and said, "This is for you. It is the queen's brooch and will serve to hold up your cloak when you are bigger. Do not lose it for it might be very useful to you one day. Suppose, for instance, you were galloping along my road another time and the men caught you and wanted to punish you— then you could show them this brooch and they would know that the queen had given you her permission to go where you wished in Iceni territory. That would be useful, wouldn't it?"

But before Marcus could answer, she said quite sternly, "Now move out of my way and let me pass, Roman."

He watched until they had gone into the shadowy hollow, then he rode off. Rudda met him half a mile farther on, where the road faded out across the moorland. His face was very pale and he said, "Did you tell her who had shown you the road and the stones?"

Marcus said scornfully, "Of course not. Romans do not do things like that. Look what she gave me."

He drew out the brooch, but Rudda put his hands over his eyes and would not look. "Put it away, put it away," he said. "It is not for me to look at. Oh, oh, this is the last time I shall go out with you! I do not think you are a lucky person to go out with. Let us go home straightway, before we meet with any more ill luck."

14

Marcus laughed and said, "There you go again, croaking like a raven."

The slave wept and beat his hands together. "You must not mention them," he said. "Oh, oh, I can see that I am doomed if I stay with you! Please let me run on and then I shall not have to listen to what you say."

So Marcus let him go and held back the white pony until the slave was well ahead. Now he felt quite certain that these Britons were the funniest people in the world.

2

The Senate's Wish

A MARRIAGE was arranged for Livia with a rich textile manufacturer of Alexandria when she was fifteen. A letter came to Marcus from his stepmother in Carthago Novo. It said: "In this life one must put duty before personal pleasure. It was your sister's wish that you should be present at the celebrations but her husband-to-be, who has the handsome name of Phrygillos and a great white villa in Athens as well as his establishment in Egypt— also a stable of twelve white horses (not to mention the finest gilded furnishings I have ever seen) together with a pleasure boat, the sail of which is of pure scarlet silk from the other side of the earth—is a busy man. His affairs require that the marriage be solemnized forthwith. No doubt you and your father the tribune will find the occasion at a later time to visit Livia in Athens or Alexandria. Then your reunion will be the more pleasurable, made in the knowledge that your private wishes were caused to wait on the exigencies of your sworn duty to Rome."

Though Marcus was seventeen when this letter came, he wept. He had never greatly liked his stepmother, who came from a harsh patrician family of Rome, but he had always dreamed of seeing his sister once more. Now, by the strange letter, he felt that Livia was lost to him forever.

For a while he stamped round his quarters in the barracks, mouthing the name Phrygillos and finding it unpleasant and cold. He felt certain that Livia was being made to marry this merchant because of his money. He could only remember her as his little friend and playmate and hated to think that she would be sent to Egypt or even Athens, into the house of a busy and, no doubt, elderly merchant.

When he went to his father's quarters to complain, the tribune smiled sadly and said, "Life has been a pleasant holiday for you until now, my son. But today you have learned that in this world we must all suffer so that the fortunes of our family shall grow."

Marcus said, "Are you prepared to sell Livia to this merchant so that my stepmother shall have villas and horses to boast of?"

Ostorius Volusenus put his great brown hand on top of his son's hand firmly and said, "Marcus, you and I are much alike, although I have never said this to you before in case I offended you. But in some ways we are not true Romans of the old patrician breed. We are of Spain, my son, where a man sets courtesy and good living above ambition. But your stepmother can claim ancient Brutus as an ancestor. She sees life differently from us. We must abide by what has been arranged."

Still Marcus would not leave the matter in this way.

16

He said, "You are the father of the family. She could have had one of the Tarquins for her ancestor, for all I care. Very well, if you disapprove, you must stop this wedding. It is clear to me, and I am not a tribune."

Ostorius Volusenus looked at him sternly then and said, "I cannot stop the wedding. It has been arranged by your grandfather, your stepmother's father, who sits in the Senate in Rome and is a close friend of the emperor himself."

Marcus said, "You are a tribune, sir. You are an officer who commands even the greatest of centurions."

Ostorius passed his hand over his brow, for the weather had turned very warm, and said, "Yes, my son, I am a tribune. But one day, when you too are a tribune, you will understand that the world would go on very well without tribunes, splendid as they may seem in their parade armor riding before the eagles. You will understand then that even tribunes have their masters, and I do not mean the legates or the generals. I mean the little, bent old men who lean on staffs to get to their seats in the Senate. One of those old men, in their gowns and with their watery eyes, can make or break a whole legion. If I stood out against this marriage, Marcus, you and I might find ourselves selling horses in Caledonia for a living afterward!"

Marcus said, "Then for the love of Mithras, let us sell horses in Caledonia—or anywhere else you can think of. I would prefer that to seeing my sister married to an old Egyptian—Greek."

Ostorius looked at him very sharply now and said, "When you have calmed down we will speak of this again. I ask only that you should consider what it is that you are so ready to throw away—our position in the legion and possibly our status as Roman citizens. And when you are thinking this over, I beg you to remember that I have known no other trade than soldiering since I

17

was your age. To me the legion is almost my mother. As for the citizenship, perhaps I could do without that—though I hardly think so, my son."

Marcus bounced out of the room in fury, but before he went through the door he turned and said, "Sir, I now see you in a new light. Always before I admired you, but now I fear that I have admired a weakling."

His father did not call him back, and when Marcus reached his own quarters he felt very miserable at having spoken so to the one man he loved. He wished that his father had beaten him for these words.

Exactly one week later a garrison-rider came to Marcus in the forum of the town and saluted. His brown face was serious as he said, "I bring bad news."

Marcus said, "You have leave to speak, soldier."

The man said, "The tribune fell in the charge at Caer Caradoc. He carried ten arrows, all of them in the front. The men stayed with him until he needed them no longer. They brought all his armor and war-gear away. It will come by wagon to you in a few days."

Marcus touched the soldier on the arm and nodded. "It was well done," he said, hoping that he would not weep until the man had saluted and turned. The legionary did this quickly and rode away. He had delivered so much bad news in his time that he knew all the signs now.

Three days later the legionary legate in Lindum sent for Marcus and said to him gently, "We mourn, too, Roman. You do not mourn alone."

Quintus Petillius Cerialis was still a young man for all his service with the ninth legion, and Marcus could somehow bear these words better from him than from an old man, who would have spoken of gods and destiny and honor. Cerialis was not like that; he said almost straightway, "Your father's gear—does it fit you, Marcus?"

The young man smiled sadly. "Yes, commander," he

said. "I seem to have grown a great deal in the last few years."

Then the legate rose from behind the many scrolls upon his table and came to Marcus, taking his hand and holding it firmly. He said, "In this lovely but strange land, most of us have to grow quickly if we are to support the burdens that are laid suddenly on our shoulders. Here, at the edge of the world, far from Rome and comfort, we must all be ready at any moment to grasp the sword that is thrown to us out of the darkness."

Marcus blinked and said, "I am not sure that I understand you, sir."

Cerialis patted him on the shoulder, then turned to the papers on his table and selected one of them which bore the seal of the Senate in Rome. He held it before the youth for a moment, then touched it with his other hand and said, "This proclamation announces that you are a tribune of the ninth legion as from this date. If your father's armor fits you, there is little more for you to worry about. You have lived here for the greater part of your life, and you know more about our military affairs than any raw tribune sent out from Rome. I regard you as the ideal choice, my boy. What more can I say?"

Marcus waited awhile then answered, "Sir, this is a very sudden appointment. How did the Senate know of my father's death so quickly that they could elect me in his place and also get word to you of their decision?"

Cerialis rolled up the scroll and smiled as he sat once more at the table. "Marcus," he said, "your grandfather is a powerful politician. It was his wish that, when the moment came, you would follow in your father's trade. It is one of your grandfather's wishes that always, while he lives, he shall have a kinsman as tribune in one or another of the legions."

Marcus felt his chin quivering. He said to still it, "So

19

this commission was waiting all the time for my father to die, sir?"

The legate raised his eyebrows and said, "You put it bluntly, tribune—but, yes! It was a precaution to preserve the continuity. Are you content now?"

For a mad second or two Marcus felt like reaching over and tearing the scroll into pieces; but then his senses came back. He stood upright and said, "Yes, sir. I am content."

Cerialis looked down at his papers and said, "You will take over your father's apartment and his command. You know all the men and the other officers. They trust you and will obey you. Have you anything to ask?"

Marcus drew back his shoulders and let his long jaw jut out. "No, sir," he said. "I have nothing to ask. Nothing at all."

Then he saluted stiffly and turned to the door. And when he had gone the legate turned to a Greek scribe who sat behind him and said, "You have just seen a boy turn into a man, Lysias. It is a way we Romans have."

The Greek bit at the end of his stylus for a while, then said with an ironic smile, "You are much like our old Spartans, sir. You know very well how to turn them into killers, but do you know how to change them back into gentle men of peace?"

Quintus Petillius Cerialis got up from his stool and thumped about the room. He said, smiling grimly, "We have only learned how to do one thing at a time, Lysias. We are not yet Greeks, my friend. But I will tell you this—the way things are going in this dark, damp island, before too long we shall have need for all the hard soldiers we can get. It will be a lifetime before the gentle men of peace you speak of come into their own in Britain."

The Greek smiled at him cynically and scratched his cheek with the point of his pen.

The legate wagged a finger at him in mock warning

and said, "Yes, you may smile, Greek, but when the fire crackles about your ears, do not forget what I have just said."

3

Sword Drill

In THE MONTHS that followed, Tigidius the centurion, the *pilus prior,* guided Marcus through all the hazards that might bring about the downfall of a newly appointed staff officer, and in many ways, treated the young man like a son. It was Tigidius who taught him sword drill with the long *spatha,* the cavalryman's weapon, on the parade ground facing a stout post as tall as a man. "No, no, lad," the centurion said, "never slash! Consider, a slash-cut rarely kills, however hard you strike out, because your enemy's vitals will be protected by his buckler, or if you can get so close, by his bones themselves. And a wounded Celt is even worse that a whole one! Once you wound one of these tribesmen he will go mad with fury and never let you be until he lies stark—or you do. Belgae and Germans are exactly the same. Hurt them, and you are begging for trouble. There is only one way to do it—keep the hilt well down and push out at their faces. They hate that!"

Marcus said drily, "That is no surprise to me, Tigidius."

The centurion glanced at him sharply, then said, "Very well, if I want to hear a comedy I go to the amphitheatre when there is a play. But now we are training, and that is never a joke. As I said, a sharp thrust at the face to bring his small shield or sword up, then with the hilt still low, a withdrawal and a quick push in lower down, below the shield. Now let me see you do it at the wooden post. And have the goodness to shout with each thrust."

Marcus wiped the sweat from his forehead and said, "Centurion, this thrusting business I can understand well, and I will do my best to follow your instructions. But this shouting seems ridiculous in a grown man. I have heard the legionaries doing it and . . ."

Tigidius said grimly, "And you think it undignified? Yes, yes, I know, lad. I have tried to train more young tribunes than I have had warm dinners. Now let me tell you this—*dignitas* is a splendid thing for officers to have *after* the fighting is over, when they go forward to browbeat the defeated chieftain, who more often than not, poor devil, is half-dead on his feet. But *dignitas* goes unnoticed in the thick of the affray itself. What is needed then is a bit of play-acting. No, do not shake your head like that; if I had a bag of gold coin for every affair I've stood up in, I should own a gladiatorial school on the Tiber now, not be beating my brains out with a young pup like you! Mark my words, there are very few heroes in this world—among Romans or Germans or Celts or Greeks; especially among Greeks, who say that it is Zeus who makes men what they are! Most men are timid at heart. Oh yes, they look brave enough once the game starts, but that's because of many things—perhaps they are angry because their homes have been burned and their children hurt; perhaps they do not want their comrades to think they are cowards; or perhaps they have been at the wine-jar before the advance started. You can never tell. There is only one thing you *can* tell, and that is that most of the men in the battle would far rather be sitting quietly by the fireside. This applies to these British, most of all. They are family men, farmers, great talkers, and so on. So, when you come against them, your first task is to make them think that you live only for the sword, only for fighting. Make them think that, and you have half-won the battle. So shout, you young hound, shout! Shout as though you are first cousin to Mars himself, as though you have wolf's blood in your veins, and as though you cut your first tooth on an enemy's shield-rim. Have you got that?"

Marcus smiled a little sadly, then said, "Yes, Tigidius. But I still think. . ."

The centurion seemed to swell to twice his size. His eyes began to push out of their lids. The rough bristles on his cheeks rose. His color changed from a gentle brown to something almost like purple. He choked a little then said, "Think? Think? By the Twelve Altars of Mithras, but when did the Senate employ a young tribune for thinking? Do you know what tribunes are? Do you know what the legionaries call them when they have ridden by? Do you? Well, do you?"

Marcus had never seen Tigidius like this before. He did not wait to hear what tribunes were; he dropped the hilt of his *spatha*, poked it out sharply at the post, then with lowered head, drew back the blade and dug it a thumb's length into the seasoned oak.

Tigidius came behind him, smiling, and said, "Here, let me draw it out for you, son. It's often easier to put them in than get them out."

He struggled awhile, withdrawing the keen blade without bending it, then he said, "I have not seen one go in that far before, I must say. Old Ostorius would have liked that. Yes, he would have been proud."

23

After that Tigidius never mentioned Marcus's father again. Nor did he ever taunt the young tribune in training him. They would march with the men in the dust for twelve hours a day, chanting the old cadence: "Sky-earth-road-stone! Sharp-steel-cuts-to-bone!" Then they would eat a supper of oat-porridge or barley-meal—but never meat—washed down with a watered wine as tart as vinegar.

Marcus once said, "I have never understood the men's taste for this sort of wine, Tigidius. I would rather drink water itself."

The centurion said quietly, "You wouldn't if you had ever campaigned in the deserts, lad. Take my word for it, an enemy on the run can do more damage with a poisoned water-well than he ever could with spear and sword. Besides, when you get the taste of it you will find this thin wine very thirst quenching. Why, if you drank a cup of the rich vintage that Cerialis keeps locked up in his cellar, your tongue would be hanging down onto your chest after you'd marched ten miles!"

Tigidius also insisted that Marcus should always go out in the usual leather gear of the infantryman. "Yes, yes," the centurion said, "I know that armor is heavier and more dignified, and so on, but when you march with the men you will get kitted out like the men; heavy boots and all. I have known tribunes who got their throats slit by their own legion behind haystacks in hard territory, for not knowing that simple thing. If you want to lead men, then suffer with them. Caligula knew that; old Cato knew it too. They weren't good men, but by Mithras, they were good soldiers. And that is what we are out to make of you. If you want to be a good man as well, then no doubt the Greek Lysias has some formula for that. He has for most things."

So Marcus sweated out his months of training in leather helmet, tunic and breeches. His feet grew calluses

24

from the thick-soled marching boots that Tigidius made him put on.

And in the end he was not only a staff officer; he was a soldier. And what was best, every man of the ninth legion knew it. Every one of them called him by his name when they met privately, though never on the parade ground.

4

First Mission

SOON AFTER MARCUS had completed his basic training and now wore his tribune's high-crested helmet with authority as he cantered about the strong garrison on the hill, a letter came to him from a vessel that had put into the river Abus to collect a cargo of hides and jet from Whitby in the north. It was from his sister Livia and its message was a short one: "Trade calls my respected husband to Palmyra in Syria. There we shall set up house. Our baby girl, Drusilla, resembles you much and daily reminds me of you. May fame and fortune visit you. May we meet again, the gods willing."

At first Marcus felt hurt that he had not heard of the baby earlier; his next feeling was one of loneliness again, for Palmyra was half a world away. But then he shrugged off this self-pity and wondered if there was any gift he might send the child by the ship that stll lay in the Abus, being loaded for the return journey.

Tigidius was with him when Marcus opened his loot-coffer and rummaged in it. There were the usual odds and ends—a cracked gorget of twisted gold, a vicious old bronze skinning-knife, a handful of tarnished Celtic coins, some pieces of rough amber, and the brooch which the queen had given him when he was a boy.

He said, "It seems that I have nothing that would amuse a baby girl, centurion. Unless I send her the brooch to wear when she grows up."

Tigidius pulled his lips tightly together and said, "If you sent that, a sailor might steal it. Or, if it got to its destination, no doubt your rich brother-in-law would despise it as rude native work, and throw it away. No, I think its place is in your box, Marcus. It might turn out to be useful to you in the end. Perhaps one day, when you travel on duty up north, you might get a village craftsman to make the child a lucky necklace of garnets and jet beads. But in the meantime there is something else that must occupy us. The legate wishes to speak to you about it now."

Quintus Petillius Cerialis was looking worried, pacing up and down his office. He did not ask Marcus to sit down but said straightway, "Tribune, I am a little disturbed. Things are not very well among the tribes."

Marcus wished to show his knowledge and said, "I don't know, sir. We had a man of the Cornavii in the garrison only yesterday, arranging for our corn supplies.

He told us how contented his people were out there in the midlands under Roman rule."

Cerialis regarded him bleakly then said, "The Cornavii will say anything when they are bargaining, tribune. I am not concerned about them, they let the wind wag their tongues about as it suits them. I am worried about the Coritani to our south and the Iceni to the east. Something is happening among them and I can't put my finger on it. They seem to be humming like a swarm of bees—but the moment they see a Roman they go silent again. I don't like it, but until I can get a reliable spy or two onto the problem, there is nothing I can do."

Marcus put on a very stiff look and said, "You are not asking me to become a spy are you, legate?"

Cerialis smiled and shook his head. "No, my boy," he said, "not that. But, make no mistake, if I found it necessary for you to go spying on behalf of Rome, I should send you—and you would go! There are not many officers here in Lindum who can look as British, and sound as British, as you can, young man."

Marcus could not decide whether the legate meant this as a compliment or not, so he said nothing but just stood to attention with his helmet under his left arm.

Then Cerialis said, "In the past three months we have lost a score of trained battle horses from the pastures outside the west wall. They are taken at night, it seems, although I have trebled the guard on the grazing sector."

Marcus said, "That seems ridiculous, legate. They are all branded with the legion's mark, and couldn't be sold again in the cattle fairs."

The commander nodded. "That is the whole point, tribune," he answered. "If they are not being stolen for the market, then why would the British want them? Our horses are useless for any other purpose than the fast charge. Show them a wagon or a chariot and they would kick it to pieces. What is your guess, man?"

27

Marcus scratched his chin and then said slowly, "Which of the tribes would want to use them in battle against us? In any case, the chiefs have their own light-built ponies that they seem to prefer."

The legate said quietly, "Let us suppose that the chiefs were getting dissatisfied with the native ponies. Let us imagine that some young chieftain, relatively close at hand, dreamed of playing us at our own game and thought of using heavy cavalry on us, for whatever reason. Who comes to your mind? Come on, speak up. You know all the local princes, or whatever they call themselves."

Marcus looked away for a while. The legate tapped impatiently on the table, so at last the tribune said, "I could name a dozen young princes. But it is not just, to name names in a case like this. One needs proof before laying charges, sir."

Quintus Petillius Cerialis gave him a most stark look, then said with difficulty, "Tribune Marcus Volusenus, I did not ask you to visit me so that I might be given a lecture on law. We can leave that to the lawyers. We are soldiers, always remember that. Very well, give me some names."

Marcus said coldly, "Under protest, sir. The most active of the princes are Gwyn son of Nudd, Cynwas son of Tringad, Osla Longsword, and Togodumnus the Younger."

The legate gazed at him for a while then nodded. "I already have them on my list, tribune," he said, smiling shrewdly. "Yes, you know the tribes, I will agree. Now of these, who is the most fond of horses?"

Marcus thought for a moment, then said, "Why, Cynwas, sir! He thinks of nothing else. He claims to have horses in his ancestry."

Now Cerialis sat down on his chair and signed for Marcus to take the stool that stood before the long table.

And when they were both seated he said, "If you were looking for Cynwas at this time of the year, where in Coritani territory would you seek him?"

Marcus said, "That is not easy, sir. These horse-herders move about a great deal to find grazing."

The legate said sharply, "I know that, tribune. I am not a fool. Come to the point. If it were a matter of life or death, where would you look for Cynwas?"

Marcus frowned and then said quite abruptly, "Beyond Ratae, where the Fosse Way cuts the Viroconium road, eight miles north of Venonae across the Trent. He keeps his best stock there."

Cerialis smiled now. "Well done, Marcus," he said. "At noon today I want you to go down there and see what sort of stock this Cynwas has tucked away over the Trent. Tigidius will go with you, mounted, and you will take that young decurion, Novantico, and his ten men. He is an ambitious fellow and deserves to see a little action if there is any going. He will make a centurion one day in my opinion. What do you think of him?"

Marcus drew his chin back and almost sulked for a while. He said, "Is this an official request, sir? If so, I will have the scribe set down my report in writing."

The legate said, "You are far too touchy this morning, tribune. Very well, if you do not wish to speak about the decurion, so be it. Sometimes a commander learns about his men from private word-of-mouth discussions, as you will find."

Marcus rose from the stool and said, "Sir, my father never spoke about his men; only to them personally, or of them officially on the army reports. It is not a soldier's business to discuss a man's character behind his back."

Cerialis forced himself to smile now and said, "I am corrected, by my newest tribune. Once again, so be it. I asked for it. But tell me one thing—do you like Novantico?"

29

Marcus stared straight ahead and said stonily, "He is a good soldier."

Then the legate said, "Very well, Marcus, I will dismiss you before you teach me more of what a general should or should not ask. May you have good luck in your mission. See that the men have adequate rations and do not let them sleep in the damp. A sick soldier is no soldier. Make them take their cloaks. I always come back with a cough when I have been along Trentside."

Marcus saluted and went out to the courtyard. The centurion was waiting for him and smiled as he said, "Did he tell you to make them wear their cloaks?"

Marcus nodded furiously. "He did," he said gruffly. "To be an officer in the ninth legion is splendid training for becoming a nursemaid when your time is up."

Tigidius put on a sympathetic face and nodded. "You take the words right out of my mouth, little one," he said. "Now go and see that your own cloak is packed properly behind your saddle."

Then Tigidius stumped off, leaning on his oak staff, to see that his servant had packed up all his gear correctly according to the manual. And that included his cloak.

5

The Men in the Wood

SOON AFTER they had left the flat water-meadows
north of the river the thirteen men lost track of any road-
ways, and came to a halt before a mass of tangled, green
woodland that seemed to creep over the billowing countryside, as though smothering it with foliage.

Novantico, the decurion, looked past Marcus, a smile
on his thin pale face and said, "Centurion, in my opinion
we should not take the men among those trees."

Tigidius looked at him from under lowered brows and
said, "Address your remarks to the tribune, soldier. He
is in command."

Novantico sniffed just audibly and replied, "I need not
repeat what I said. The tribune will have heard my words."

Then Tigidius went up to him quite slowly and said,
"I am a patient man, soldier. So I will tell you again—
address your remarks to the tribune."

Novantico was about to answer in annoyance, but
just then the centurion dug down with his oak staff and
leaned on it heavily. The decurion flinched, flung back
his head and stifled a groan. Then he collected himself

and said, "Sir, ought we to take the men through the woods where there might be an ambush?"

Marcus stared over the man's head and said, "I know the people here. We shall proceed according to orders."

When they went on, the decurion was limping quite painfully. None of the legionaries offered to carry his shield and spear for him, however.

Tigidius, riding at the front with Marcus, whispered quietly, "It's all right. He will settle down before we get back to Lindum. He's too ambitious, that's all. We will train him, you and I."

It was a sultry day and gnats swarmed under the overhanging branches of oak and alder and ash. The men sweated with their heavy packs. The two horsemen soon found that it was easier to walk beside their mounts because of the boughs; but Tigidius called out a warning to all that they should keep clear of bracken and old heaps of sticks in case there were adders nesting in them.

At the bottom of a sandstone gully they came on a wide pool of dark water. It was green-scummed with mosses, but the men were so thirsty that three of them broke ranks and ran down to it. Tigidius bawled out, "Keep away from that water, you fools."

Novantico glared and said quite loudly, "Centurion, who is to give the orders here?"

The centurion drew a deep breath and said, "I am sorry, decurion. But it was an urgent case. We don't want them down with water-sickness so early on in the mission."

Novantico drew himself up stiffly and said, "Thank you, centurion. I shall put this in my report to the legate when we return."

Tigidius lost his temper a little and said, "You can have it engraved in letters of gold for all I care, fellow. These men have cost good money and time to train. I will not have them wasted needlessly."

32

The decurion said, "Are you alleging that I am indifferent to the health of the men, centurion? If so, I would like you to say so before the tribune as a witness."

Suddenly Marcus flared up and said, "This is not a school for dancers, soldier. Keep your tantrums for another place and let us get on with our work."

Novantico half-turned as though he meant to ask the legionaries to bear witness for him. But he suddenly realised that they were all looking away, or pretending to catch butterflies and gnats; so he shrugged his narrow shoulders and then saluted ironically. "I am at your command, sir," he said.

The centurion answered, "Of course you are. That is what Rome pays you for. Now start the men off again and they shall have a measure of marching-wine at the end of three miles. But no more water. That is an order."

Then all at once, as the squad moved away, there was a quick rustling in the thorn bushes beyond the pool. The men fell flat to the turf, swinging their heavy squarish shields over their heads in case a flight of arrows followed the noise. Marcus sprang away from his horse so that it should not be shot in any attempt to hit him, and dived behind a flat stone that would hardly have protected a hedgehog.

Novantico did not fall with the men, but slinging his shield before him, pounded with his javelin at the ready into the thorns. Tigidius shouted out to him, but he did not seem to hear.

He was back within a count of twenty, dragging a flaxen-haired girl of about twelve, who was striking at him and trying to kick him with her bare feet. He almost flung her toward the tribune and said, "Here is the enemy, sir."

Marcus got up from the stone and said, "I see only a little girl, decurion."

She wore a long, shapeless robe of grey wool, tied

round the waist with a thong of untanned leather. Her light grey eyes were wide with anger and her russet face screwed up. About her neck swung a clumsy amulet of iron, looped onto a cord of cow-hair.

Marcus beckoned her to him and said in Celtic, "Who are you? Are you all right? He did not hurt you, did he?"

The girl gazed at him for a moment then answered in stiff Latin, "It would take more than that beanpole to hurt me. If my brother Cynwas had seen him with his hand in my hair, that Roman would be shorter by a head's length now. I am Aranrhod. Who are you?"

The Tribune answered, "I am Marcus Volusenus, son of Ostorius."

Then she began to laugh and to show her even white teeth. "What funny names you all have!" she said. "Our names are so easy to say—but you take a delight in having names that no one can say."

Marcus said, "That is a matter of opinion, lady."

Aranrhod gazed at him then and said, "Are you a Roman, though? You sound like a man of the Coritani. Are you British?"

Marcus smiled and shook his head. He said, "I have lived here most of my life, lady. You were away with your kinsfolk in Deva when I visited your tribe last. That is why you do not know me."

She said, "I saw you all fall down. You thought there would be arrows next, didn't you? Cynwas will laugh when I tell him."

Marcus answered, "And I shall tell Cynwas to make his sister wash her hands and face before she goes out into the woods wandering."

She looked down at her hands and said, "I dropped my lizard and got dirty trying to find him under the bushes. I love my lizard, just as you love your horse. I saw you jump away from him so that he should not be hit."

The centurion came closer then, and said gently to the girl, "Has Cynwas got horses, princess? Has he got some new horses?"

She stared at the centurion boldly and then shook her mane of yellow hair and shrugged her thin shoulders. "Perhaps he has and perhaps he hasn't," she answered. "You must ask Cynwas. I am not the chief."

Marcus said, "We will do that, happily, if you will take us to him."

The girl suddenly sat down on the stone that Marcus had tried to use as a shelter, and drew a small green lizard from inside her robe. It stayed motionless on her bare arm for a second or two, then all at once it ran up onto her shoulder and down her back. She twisted round, as fast as a snake, and caught the little creature before it could drop to the ground. Then she smiled at Marcus and said, "See, he is a very lively fellow. He needs all my care and attention. I am his mother now because he is the only one left of his family. One of the new horses trod on his nest and killed the others. So it is my duty to care for him."

Tigidius leaned over and said, "The new horses, Aranrhod? What color are they?"

The British girl pursed her lips and frowned at the centurion. She said severely, "You are an inquisitive man, aren't you? Do I ask if you have a new cloak and what color it is?"

Novantico stepped forward then and said sharply, "Leave her to me for a few minutes, centurion. I will make her talk sense."

Tigidius turned to him slowly and said, "Do you understand what such information would cost us, soldier? Do you know what Cynwas would do if he thought we had laid hands on his sister? I can tell you, the ninth legion would have empty beds for thirteen men by dawn tomorrow. Now stand away from her, and remember your place."

The decurion started with shock at this and said, "They are Britons, sir, not Romans. You treat them as though they were Romans."

Tigidius nodded and answered, "Yes, and you may put that in your report also when you get back to camp. It just happens that you have manhandled a princess of the royal house in these parts. It also happens that this little girl, who struck fear into us all with her game, will be considered as being of greater importance to her kinsfolk than the whole of the ninth legion. And if we have the good fortune to stand before Cynwas, I would like you to remember that he and his sister are noblefolk. I have yet to hear that anyone named Novantico has ever risen above the rank of municipal road-sweeper at Camulodunum."

The decurion flushed and clenched his teeth. He stepped back to the men and began to form them into squad, speaking to them roughly.

Aranrhod said smiling, "I understood all you said, centurion. I know camp Latin too!"

Marcus took her by the hand and said, "Very well, we have no secrets from you, and that is good because we are all friends here. Now will you take us to where Cynwas is?"

She got up from the stone and did a little dance, all by herself, her long bedraggled skirt and yellow hair flying out behind her. Then she stopped and said, "Does Cynwas want to see you? Have you important business with him? He is very busy with the other chiefs just now."

Marcus put on a serious face and said, "In a way, Tigidius and I are chiefs also, and we would like to talk to Cynwas about important things."

Aranrhod thought for a time, then said, "If I do not lead you to him, you will never find Cynwas. That is worth something, is it not?"

Novantico snorted and said loudly, "There, they are

36

all the same! Beggars, all of them. And you call them noblefolk!"

Marcus ignored him and said to the girl, "Yes, it is worth something. What is the price, lady? But do not ask for too much, because we have not come bearing gifts today."

She looked him up and down with a strange smile on her face and said, "This is the price; let all the men swing their swords behind their backs and give their spears to one man to carry. Then it will be seen that you come in peace; that is the price."

Marcus glanced at the centurion, who nodded. "Very well, lady," he said. "We will pay that price. But do you swear that we shall be taken to see Cynwas?"

She did a few more steps of the dance then, and said, "Of course you will. I have said so, haven't I?"

Marcus sat her on his saddle and they led the straggling column. The man with the spears walked at the tail end.

When they had gone down a long winding path covered with rotting beech leaves and overgrown with ferns, Aranrhod suddenly pointed with her forefinger up the slippery slope toward a small grove of oaks. "There is a man in there," she said. "He is a man of the Iceni, a very fierce warrior."

Marcus whispered, "How long has he been there? What does he want?"

She shrugged and said, "Two days, but I don't think he wants anything. He is just there. I saw him when I was running after my lizard."

Novantico immediately broke from the column and raced up the slope. They saw him push through the lower boughs of the oak screen, then come back with his hand over his mouth looking paler than ever.

He slid down the slope again and said, "He is there all right, hanging from a branch by a noose!"

Marcus looked very severely at Aranrhod and said,

"That was not a pleasant trick to play, lady. Well-mannered girls do not jest like that."

She said loftily, "You can tell that to Cynwas. I am not interested. No, I am very bored with you all. Let us be on our way. You must all go through that little tunnel of thorns. There is no other way. I shall not speak to you any more for the moment. I am displeased with you all now."

They did as she said and went, bending low to get through the dark tunnel of leaves. And when all of them were through except the man carrying the javelins, twenty Celts wearing helmets and war-shirts rose up from the ferns, with drawn swords in their hands.

Aranrhod kicked the horse along and drew away from the skirmishing. She shouted back to Novantico, "Let this be a lesson to you, beanpole!"

One of the tallest of the Britons came forward and said, "Unfasten your sword belts, all of you. Do not hesitate, we do not wish to kill you, yet. When, is for Cynwas to decide."

Tigidius said wryly, "Do as he says, men. And from this time on, never let me hear any of you boasting of our Roman wisdom. That little girl and her lizard are the equal of thirteen picked men of the ninth legion."

Novantico was biting his knuckles and glowering about him desperately. A Celt wearing a blue cloak and leather breeches took him easily by the arm and pushed him forward. "Move," he said. "You wanted to visit Cynwas, and so you shall!"

6

Cynwas

THE GIRL had been right; no one could have found Cynwas without a guide. His Dun stood, partly hidden by creeping plants and brushy undergrowth, halfway up a steep sandstone slope, and was largely formed by the roots of the many trees that flourished on the ridge-top. The clan of Coritani that Cynwas ruled now that his father, Tringad, was dead had so skilfully used the tree roots, interweaving and plaiting them together, that a great nest of basketwork had been formed, like the hanging homes of house martins or of wild bees; and this nest, now covered by mosses and lichens so that it seemed like a part of the rock face bulging outwards, was the fortress hiding-place of the chieftain and his most trusted henchmen.

Only Marcus and the centurion were allowed to scramble up the sandstone slope; the rest of the Romans were made to sit on the ground with their hands on their heads, each one guarded by a tribesman holding a naked sword. Novantico took it very badly, but the man in charge of him tapped him lightly on the neck with the flat of his blade and said, "Why do you twist your face about so, decurion? Is it beneath your digntiy to sit upon the ground? I have led a hundred men in my day, yet I would sit upon the ground. You have command of ten poor fellows—and you frown! In my right hand I hold the cure to all frowning. Have you looked at it?"

Novantico raised his eyes and stared at the sword. He

said after a while, "It looks well enough, for native work. It is too heavy at the point, however. A good sword should come broad from the hilt toward the point, lightening as it goes. So, the thrust is balanced and the aim accurate."

The Celt considered this and nodded; his heavy plaits swung against his cheeks. He said, "You are not wrong, decurion. But we use them differently. See . . ."

He snatched a crab apple from an overhanging bough and with the same movement tossed it into the air. As it came down, red in the sunlight, his long blade flashed out and the small fruit fell, evenly divided, before the decurion, who picked it up and examined it closely.

"You have a good eye," he said. "I once saw a Batavian who did much the same—but he threw up a grape and cut it crosswise too. It fell in four parts."

The Celt smiled and said, "One hears of these Batavians and their grapes. I have heard of a Frisian who did it with an axe, only he used a walnut. If all such men would only agree to join together—what a warband! Hey, Roman, what a warband!"

Novantico turned his head and spoke no more to the man; but he did not frown any more either.

Up in the Dun, Marcus and the centurion stood before Cynwas. He was a very big man with red hair, who sat upon a flat stone with a length of thick tartan over his head and shoulders, sneezing. He said to Marcus, "Forgive me, friend, but I have caught one of these Trentside colds. This always happens to me when I come here for the grazing. Do you catch colds on that draughty hill at Lindum?"

Marcus said, "Up there we live in stone houses and have underfloor heating. If we take cold we treat it with mulled wine flavored with spices. One sweats through the night, but in the morning the cold has gone."

Cynwas said, "My father used to carry a hare's foot slung round his neck to ward off colds; but it never

40

worked. He suffered through the winter, I can assure you. If the truth was known, that is what took him off at the end."

Marcus said, "No, it was that spear gash he got on your last big cattle raid against the Brigantes. He did not take care of himself. I saw that wound, if you recall, and I can tell you that if a legionary got one like that he would be put into the garrison hospital for a month. But Tringad was out hunting deer a week after he was wounded. You folk don't look after yourselves; that is your trouble."

Cynwas smiled up at him slyly and said, "We have many troubles, friend. As for looking after ourselves— well, I grant you, at one time we didn't. It was one of our rules never to bandage a fresh wound until it had been exposed for a day and a night. By that time, most of the sufferers needed no further treatment. But we are learning, Marcus; yes, we are learning."

The tribune waited awhile before saying, "Yes, you are learning, friend, but perhaps not fast enough. It is hardly wise to take branded horses from the legion's fields, would you say?"

Cynwas sat back and gazed at the Roman very steadily. Then he smiled and nodded with quiet scorn. He said at last, "I thought that you did not visit me out of friendship, Volusenus. I thought there was something else that brought you here. Well, I will tell you. If you were to climb to the top of the rise, you would see four horses bearing the Roman brand grazing in the pastures below among my own beasts."

Tigidius said gently, "We are looking for twenty, not four, Cynwas."

The Briton turned to him stony-faced and said, "The legion must look elsewhere for the others then. The Iceni who came through my territory drove only four. If he could speak now, he would tell you that, no doubt; but after my men took him to the wood he stopped talking.

41

As for your four horses, they are in better condition now than they were when we took them into our care. Your grooms would have been pleased with them when we returned them."

Marcus said, "You speak as though you mean to keep them, Cynwas. That would be a mistake, friend. Look, I should not have accused you so rashly, and I am sorry indeed. But you must not keep those horses. You will be paid in full for their care and grazing, of course."

Cynwas blew down his nose as though smoke had got into it and said, "Must! Must not! Can you Romans use no other words? You come to my house and accuse me of being a horse-thief; then, when you hear the truth, you say that you are sorry and expect that all will be well again. How long have you known me, tribune?"

Marcus shrugged his shoulders helplessly. "Almost ten years," he said.

The Briton nodded and said, "And in those ten years have you ever known me put my hand on anything that belonged to you, or that bore the Roman mark?"

The tribune held out his hands. "Look," he said, "I am sorry, Cynwas. I am sorry down to the heart—what more can I say? It appeared that you must have taken the horses."

Now Cynwas rose and said coldly, "Just as it appeared that you were once my friend, tribune. But now it seems that if my tribe want friends they must go to their own people for them, and not to Romans."

Tigidius spoke then and said, "You are angry, Cynwas, and you do not mean what you have just said. Angry men speak in haste; let us not throw fuel on the fire."

Cynwas suddenly turned to the henchmen who stood about the secret hall and signaled to them with his hand. They went out grumbling and left him alone with the Romans. For some moments he stared at them hard, then sat down again and pointed his long forefinger at the centurion. "You," he said, "you talk to me of throwing fuel on fires. Do you know what fuel has been thrown on the fire at Venta Icenorum? Or do your commanders not tell their centurions of the high policies that the Senate in Rome dabbles with?"

Marcus said, "No more of this cat and mouse game, Cynwas. Have the goodness to speak straight sense to us. We are plain soldiers. We do not hear every little bit of gossip that spreads through the tribes."

Cynwas smiled bitterly and said, "I was wondering when you would tell me that you were plain soldiers. Romans always say that when their leaders have led them into difficulties, as though that cleared them of all guilt, as though that justified all cruelty."

The centurion became impatient then and said, "This is wild talk, Cynwas. Why don't you get the bard to set it to harp music? It would go well."

But Marcus shook his head at the centurion and said, "What guilt and what cruelty are you speaking of, Cynwas? Am I guilty and cruel, because I come under orders looking for twenty stolen horses? If you lost such horses, would you not go looking for them? I know you too well, old friend! You would be out with forty men at your back and torches ready to burn down whole villages, in vengeance for horse-stealing."

Cynwas said in a cold voice, "We are not talking of horses now, tribune. We are talking of Romans. We are talking of what your people have just done, in the name of justice, at Venta Icenorum. And it took many more than forty of them to do it, the cowardly ravens."

Suddenly he brought his fist down hard onto a clay lamp, smashing it to fragments and sending the oil spattering across the dim room. Marcus wiped his hand down the front of his tunic and said, "It was a shame to ruin such a pretty lamp, friend. But now that you have done it, perhaps we can hear some sense from you. Tell us what is troubling you, for I swear to Mithras we do not know."

43

Now Cynwas spoke with passion, his face as red as though he had been standing in the north wind for an hour. "Very well," he said, "you ask and you shall hear. Three days ago your people put the torch to Venta Icenorum. They dragged the queen and her daughters from the house, strung them up on posts, and flogged them with whips in the sight of all their people."

Marcus stared at him wide-eyed. "But the queen was in mourning for her dead husband, Prasutagus," he said. "It is not our custom to dishonor mourning widows and their kinsfolk. Someone must have brought the wrong news, Cynwas."

The chieftain said, "My nephew brought the news. Do you now accuse my kinsfolk of being liars? No, the news is true enough, Roman. It is your ears that cannot bear to hear the truth. Since you are so ill-informed, let me tell you the story; then you may call me a liar again if you wish, though I do not think you will. Queen Boadicea knew well enough that as soon as her husband breathed his last you vultures, Nero's scavengers, would be into the palace, rummaging among the treasure-chests for all you could lay hands on. She was no fool. We Celts are not fools; we are realists, whatever you high and mighty fellows with your half-understood Greek philosophy may think. No, do not sneer at me! I am serious. Hear me out."

Marcus made a little bow of the head and clenched his jaws. "Go on," he said then.

Cynwas stared him in the eye. "I shall," he said. "The time for politeness is over, soldier. Now, in my house, you will listen while I speak. I repeat, the queen knew that, in order to keep what little your tax-gatherers have left her family, she must prevent the grave-robbers of Rome from rushing in and stealing all when her husband died. And so, to protect her two daughters and herself, she publicly named your emperor, that fat-bellied drunkard Nero, as the coheir to all her husband left."

Marcus said drily, "That is an old trick, Cynwas. Our own noblemen do it to avoid death duties. It often comes out cheaper that way."

The Briton thumped his fist against his own stomach in anger. "Comes cheaper!" he said. "Why, man, you use words like a Syrian market-haggler. Cheaper? We are not goods to be bought and sold. We are free men. Our history is longer than your own. We were lords and warriors when your folk groveled in the fields with your plowsticks for the Etruscans. We wore gold at our wrists and throats when your fathers had nothing more than a gaggle of frightened geese to give the alarm over your reed-huts, down by the river you call the Tiber. Cheaper? Why, you had a cheap enough army to guard Rome in those days. But you had a dear enough payment to make when our kinsman Brennus pushed into your city with his Gauls, and weighed the tribute out in his iron scales. You had a dear enough payment when our kinsman Vercingetorix took Caesar by the nose and . . ."

Marcus walked up to him and stroked his cheek with a hard soldier's hand. He said, "Cynwas, brother, you are frothing at the mouth. Take my neckcloth and wipe your face."

Suddenly all the red of violence went from the Briton's cheeks. The sky-blue of his eyes came back as when the sun shines again from behind a rain cloud. He reached out and gripped the Roman by the right ear and tugged hard at it in the sort of friendship that one lion might feel for another. He said, "You are a fool, Marcus. You are a fool with such wisdom that one day we may have to kill you. A man can only stand a little sense at a time. I pray to the gods that my hand is not chosen to put the sword to you."

Just then Aranrhod ran in, her tawny hair all tangled and her gold neck-ring bobbing up and down on the faded grey stuff of her gown. She was muddied from hem to forehead, but she was laughing. "Cynwas," she shouted,

45

"I put the Roman's horse at the stockade below Prysg field and he took it without a falter. Can I have the horse?"

Cynwas made a stern face, then glanced over her head at Marcus. "I am sorry," he said. "My sister lives for horses. She dreams of them by day and by night. She would eat their fodder and sleep in their stables if I would let her."

Marcus smiled a little stiffly. "It is in the blood," he said. Then he turned to the girl and put his hand on her shoulder. "Princess," he said gently, "your brother cannot give you my horse. Only I could do that."

At first she turned on him frowning and shrugging off his hand. Then she thought a little and began to smile. "Tribune," she said, "I beg your pardon. I had forgotten it was your horse. I forget things like that."

The two men gazed down at her very solemnly. She shifted from one foot to the other and put the end of her plait into her mouth and bit it, looking very miserable. At last she said, her face screwed up, "I did not notice that you were here when I came in, tribune."

Cynwas said, "That was because the tribune is so small. He is only the length of six feet, and another foot with his helmet on. Who could expect you to notice anyone as small as that, my sister?"

She began to fidget and tug at her neck-ring. She said, "Tribune, this ring is of ancient gold. Will you take it for your horse?"

Marcus bowed gravely to her and said, "There is no lady I would rather trade with—but the horse is not mine. He belongs to Rome. He comes from the garrison stables. You might as well ask me for my sword."

She swung round and began to shout again at her brother; but he held his hand over her mouth and said, "Sister, you heard the tribune. It is not good manners to appeal to me now; also, might I tell you that it is not good manners to wriggle your finger in your ear the way

46

you do, or to go about without shoes? Besides, your feet need washing. Go to your bower and attend to that before we eat together. And tell the women to scrub them well."

Aranrhod ran out of the room, her hair flying and her torn skirts flapping against her dusty legs.

Cynwas said, "It is strange to think that one day she will marry some Pict or Scot and be a queen."

Marcus answered, "With her love for horses, what a queen of Ireland she would make! Their bards would sing such poems of her, that in the years to come men would think she had been a goddess, brother. With that golden hair and those sea-blue eyes. . . Yes, a goddess!"

Cynwas frowned a little, then said, "I will try to arrange it, tribune. But we were talking of something nearer to us than goddesses. I was telling you that Boadicea wished to share her husband's estate with Nero. But now Nero's chief vulture, the Procurator Decianus Catus, has claimed everything; not only that which belonged to Boadicea but to all her kinsfolk—the whole royal clan. All of them are beggared, all of them outlawed. And, worse than that, their queen dishonored—her house burned, and she and her daughters flogged in the square by the common executioner."

Marcus bit his lips. "If the General Suetonius were here," he said, "this Decianus Catus would need a slave to feed him for the rest of his days."

The red came back to the cheeks of the Briton. He said, "It would be one vulture picking the bones of another, the greater vulture preying on the lesser for his own profit."

The Roman stood up again. "Suetonius is a great man," he said. "He is my commander-in-chief. It is to him that my oath stands, not to Nero."

Cynwas waved his hands. "Words, words, words!" he sneered. "This Suetonius of yours at this moment is on the island of Mona with his thousands of brutes; destroying our sacred groves there, drowning our priests in the salt

47

marshes and butchering the harmless folk who still hold to the worship of their fathers. I hear that the Romans are so weary of lifting their spears that now, to save themselves labor, they rope a whole family together and fling them into the sea."

Marcus waited awhile, blowing down his nostrils. Then he said, "Cynwas, you and I are only men. We are not gods. We cannot change the world. Why should you blame me for what Rome does? I am not Rome, I am a single man, a soldier."

Suddenly the Briton smiled. It was not a happy smile, but it was the smile for which Marcus had been waiting. He took Cynwas by the hand and said nothing.

And at last the Celt said in a lowered voice, "Let us go to the table and eat together, brother."

He said the last word almost shyly, as though it was an old forgotten word that had been learned again. It made Marcus happier than he would have been at regaining all the horses of the ninth legion.

7

The Rain

THAT NIGHT the rain came down, as though it had never fallen before over the green midland countryside. It beat on the thatch of the hall and made everyone restless. Then it made its way in through a place where the reeds were thinnest, and ran down in little waterspouts, wetting the floor. Some of the Romans from the south of Spain shivered and grumbled, pulling their heavy riding-cloaks over their heads. But the tribesmen laughed at them and told them to move a little way up toward the hearth-fire where it was drier.

Novantico's face was sour. He said bitterly, "It is a place where only green frogs could live, this Britain. How could any but savages tolerate this weather?"

Cynwas came up to him and patted him on the cheek. "There, there, little one," he said in good humor, "do not fret so. Our wind and rain will make a man of you yet."

The Coritani were standing round, their russet faces gleaming with wet, their light eyes laughing to see how miserable a rainstorm had made these proud Romans in their cloaks and war-gear. Novantico swung round on them and said, "Only madmen grin at the truth. If you were in Rome, we would put you all in a play, with wooden collars round your necks and chains on your ankles, to amuse the people with your antics. I have seen apes from Egypt who were more like men."

Cynwas did not smile now, but put his hands behind his back and gripped one with the other tightly, as though he did not trust what they might do. Then he said very slowly, "You are a little man with a big temper. That is not good, unless you are a general and have power enough to back up all your words. Be at peace now and do not work yourself up into more frenzy, or it will spoil your appetite when the food comes in."

He began to turn away but Novantico suddenly reached out and grasped him by the sleeve, almost dragging him round. "Appetite?" he shouted. "Appetite for the sort of pigswill that you folk gobble down? And as for generals, do not mention your generals to me, Briton. You had one once, and his name was Caratacus. Do you recall what we did to him? Do you recall that we chased him half over his own land, and then dragged him in chains to Rome, like an orchard-robber or a cattle-thief?"

For a while Cynwas stared in astonishment. Then his hands came from behind his back and he began to reach for his dagger. And at that moment the centurion Tigidius crossed the room in two long paces, and struck Novantico a blow with a clenched fist that tumbled him into the hay on the floor.

Then he turned to the Celt and said, "That is something I should have done before, sir. I will see that he does not trouble you again."

He ordered two legionaries to drag the man out and put him into one of the huts. Cynwas watched all this in silence. His face had gone very white and his hands were trembling, but he bowed his head slightly toward Tigidius and said, "Small dogs will yelp at big ones, whatever their breed. Let us forget it; I will call in the serving-women."

Trestle-tables of oak were set up and benches dragged into the hall. Cynwas sat at the center of the narrow board with his sister on his right hand and Marcus on his left. Tigidius sat opposite his tribune, with the legionaries on one side of him and the tribesmen on the other. The women ran in with bowls of red earthenware which they filled with oat-porridge, flavored with wild honey. Then, before the great wooden platter of mutton was set before the chieftain, other women poured out sweet sticky mead into horn cups, or tart ale for those who preferred it. Tigidius said, "If our garrison cooks could bake bread half as kind to the teeth as yours, sir, we should be lucky men. But they are all from Spain, where the bread is hardly different from the stones of the dry riverbeds."

Cynwas smiled again now and said, "Then at least there is something we can teach Rome, if it is only the baking of bread."

That was a strange moment; a little silence in which all men along the feast-board stopped eating and drinking and turned their eyes toward their leaders, as though they thought the quarrel might flare up again. Marcus felt the hairs on his neck stiffen and a breath of chilly air

50

pass down his back, as though someone had walked over his grave.

Suddenly he leaned forward and unbuckled a medallion that swung at the front of his breastplate. It was as round as a man's palm and its rich gold surface glimmered in the torchlight. With a smile he reached before Cynwas and laid this medallion beside the wooden bowl from which Aranrhod was eating. "Here, lady," he said. "It has been in my mind to give you this for the last hour. Perhaps it will lessen your sadness about the horse. Or, if you choose, you could buy two horses with it. Will you accept it from me?"

At first Cynwas put out his hand as though to push the ornament back to the Roman; then he stopped and said quietly, "Well, sister, answer the tribune yourself. You are old enough to make other decisions, it seems."

Aranrhod had a piece of bread in her mouth and tried to swallow it so quickly that she began to splutter and to go red in the face. Cynwas slapped her on the back so hard that her golden plaits swung into her porridge-bowl, and then everyone began to laugh. So the bad moment passed.

And when she had finished coughing, Aranrhod touched the moulded surface of the medallion and said, "It is very beautiful. What is it? Does it carry magic in it, tribune?"

Marcus pretended to scratch his chin. "I do not know its history, lady," he said. "My father always wore it, and I think his father before him. I do not remember anyone ever saying that it held magic in it though."

The girl ran her forefinger over the design, tracing it carefully in the flickering light. She said at last, "I think that it must be a magic thing. See, it shows a god with horns upon his head."

The tribesmen lower down the board began to suck in their breath and to stare at one another. Marcus said in

51

haste, "No, lady, not a god. I think it is meant to be one of the great captains in olden times. Perhaps it is Alexander who marched all the way to India, and fought with Persians and Egyptians."

Aranrhod looked puzzled. "Then why does he wear horns?" she asked.

Tigidius saw the look in the tribune's eyes, so he said quickly, "They are not horns, lady, they are the two branches of a laurel crown. But they are now so worn with age and use that perhaps they look like horns in this light."

Cynwas stared at him and said, "I think you are the sort of man who would speak the truth to a child." It was said like a question, and Tigidius answered, his face very stiff, "Chieftain, I try to speak the truth to anyone, child or not. Few people who know me ever ask that question."

Cynwas did not answer him, but turned to his sister and said, "You are a lucky girl, lady. You must hang this pretty warrior on a leather thong and always wear it round your neck. One day, who knows, you may be a queen in India or those other places the centurion has mentioned, and then the folk there will think all the more highly of you for wearing such an emblem."

No more was said, but as soon as she could, Aranrhod left the feasting and the men drank more mead and ale from the horns and cups.

Cynwas whispered to Marcus, "She will dream all night of this. No doubt, even now the medallion will be passing from hand to hand in the maidens' bower; and every one who holds it will be making up some mad story or another about it. Come, Romans, let me fill your cups again. On a rainy night like this there is little left for us to do but sit by the warm fire and enjoy the sweet mead."

8

The Dream

THAT NIGHT, lying curled in his cloak by the dying
fire and with the rain still thudding on the roof above him,
Marcus had a strange dream. He thought that he was in a
dark forest at evening-time, with the rain rustling in the
branches above him, and the damp leaves beneath his feet
silencing all footsteps. From time to time he called into the
dusk, "Father! Father! Where are you? I want to tell you
something."

He felt very sad as he said this, and at first did not
know why. Then he remembered in his dream that he
had given away the gold medallion. And suddenly a
hoarse whispering voice came out of a hawthorn bush to him
and said, "Why are you weeping, Roman? A man does
not weep; he takes action when he is sad. A fine tribune
such as you should take action, or how shall you keep
the respect of the gods that watch over you?"

Marcus gazed around, but could see no one in the
bush. So he said into the darkness, "What action should
I take? And who are you to tell me this?"

The forest seemed to be filled with mocking laughter
then, and this time the voice came from over his head,
in the thickness of the oak leaves. It said, "I am the voice
of the earth, Roman. I live in the soil and the trees and the
hissing barley. I live in the red foxglove and the little
fishes of the streams. I live in the horn of the bull and
the hoof of the deer. Now do you know who I am?"

Marcus shook his head and said, "I do not know you. Come out and let me see you. Are you a man or a woman?"

A great wind arose and flung him against the damp green bole of an oak tree. Then the voice said from under his feet, "Now do you know who I am, Roman? Who else could throw you so hard against that tree?"

Marcus tried to wrap his cloak about him, but the wind dragged it from his fingers and he could not hold it. He said, struggling, "I have heard your voice before. I have known it since I was a little boy, but I cannot remember whose voice it is. Who are you, tell me?"

A low branch, caught in the wind, swept across his face like a savage blow, and while he reeled from it the voice said again, "How dare you ask, you foolish fellow! Do you not carry my brooch in your pouch to remind you? Have you forgotten the great stones and the riders in the sunken lane so soon? Have you forgotten the queen with hair like a fox?"

Then in his dream Marcus fell to his knees on the wet ground and said, "Forgive me, Boadicea. I have never forgotten you; not in all these years."

And the voice, coming from behind him said, "Nor have I forgotten you, my fine fellow. I shall know you again, never fear. I never forget a face, however many years pass by. I never forget a trespasser in my lane, Roman."

Marcus said, "I do not know what to do, queen. I am lost in this dark forest. I have lost my father and the golden medallion he left to me. What should I do, lady? What action should I take?"

Then the high laughter seemed to fade away, over the tree tops, on the wind, leaving everything very still and frightening. Even the rain stopped coming down. And as Marcus stared about him in wonder, a little green snake with brown markings down its back slithered close by his knees, then suddenly burrowed swiftly out of sight into the leaves before him.

Then the voice came back out of the small round hole that the creature had made, and whispered like a hiss, "Put your hand under the leaves, Roman. Dare to feel under the leaves and you will find all you have lost. That is the action you must take, brave warrior!"

Marcus was so angry at being taunted like this, he drew back his sleeve and plunged his hand down among the damp brown leaves and began to feel about. For a while he found nothing, then all at once his fingers came on something hard and cold. But it was not the medallion, nor could he drag it up to the surface however much he pulled at it.

Then a cold sweat broke out over all his body as he realised what it was he had found.

He cried out in anger and sadness, "You have tricked me, woman. My father is below the leaves. I would know that ring on his finger anywhere, though I cannot see it."

He was still shouting out and struggling when his eyes opened and he saw Tigidius above him, staring down at him with wide eyes.

"Be still, Marcus, be still!" the centurion was saying. "You are all wet, as though you had a fever. You have been dreaming some bad dream. But the time for dreaming is over. There are things to be done now that cannot wait."

The centurion took his hand from the tribune's mouth. Marcus sat up shivering and looked about him. It was broad daylight and the sun was coming in through the window-holes of the hall. The fire had burned down to white ashes and no servants had built it up again. Two legionaries were standing at the far end of the hall, looking white-faced and afraid. Outside there was much shouting in the Celtic tongue, and horses seemed to be stamping about, as though their riders were swinging them round, this way and that.

Marcus said, "What is going on, man? What has happened?"

But before the centurion could answer, Cynwas burst into the hall with his hair flying. He was dragging like a madman at the buckle of his sword-belt in order to fasten it.

"I'll tell you what has happened," he said. "Rome has betrayed us once again, my friend. That is what has happened."

Now Marcus stood up and passed his hand across his damp face. "I was asleep," he said. "I do not understand, brother. How has Rome betrayed you?"

Cynwas stormed up to him, as though he would strike him in the face. Then he seemed to hold himself back and hissed, "Your brave decurion has left in the night and has taken most of the Romans with him. All you have left now are these two, who stand trembling here like bullocks who smell the butcher coming. And I swear by Mabon, the butcher *will* come if Aranrhod is not returned to me."

Marcus gasped, "What! The men have deserted and have taken your sister with them? This cannot be true. No, it cannot be true."

One of the soldiers stepped forward a pace then and said in a dead voice, "Sir, it is true. We saw them creep out and heard them gallop away. We did not know what to do. We reported to the centurion, but it was too late then. They had gone."

Tigidius nodded gravely. "I tried to wake you, Marcus," he said, "but it was as though you lay under a deep spell."

Marcus glowered about him, then nodded. "I think I was," he said. "And the dream has not left me yet. I cannot see clearly. I can scarcely understand the words that are said to me."

Then Cynwas took him roughly by the shoulder and shook him. "The sooner you break from your dream the better, Roman," he said, "for there is blood to be paid now. The guard at Aranrhod's door lies stark with your decurion's knife in his back. My sister has been dragged

56

from her house. Our horses have been stolen. What price shall be paid for all that, do you think, tribune?"

Marcus drew away from him and gazed at the two soldiers. "Can you men ride?" he asked coldly. They nodded. "Then," he said, "if we mount without losing more time and take the road to Lindum, we may still cut off these mutinous dogs before more harm is done."

Cynwas stared at him without belief for an instant, then suddenly he said, "I do believe that you are an honest man at heart, Roman. Come, there shall be ponies for the four of you and we will take the road you say. But, when we catch these murdering thieves, do not think to save them with any Roman arguments. They shall suffer the punishment of our people, and nothing you can say shall save them."

Tigidius stepped forward and said then, "There will be no argument, Cynwas. But you will not punish them— I shall. And their punishment will be according to the law of men and not of beasts."

For a moment Cynwas was speechless. Then he said through clenched teeth, "Very well, centurion. Very well. But if my sister is not returned to me unharmed, then you too shall share the punishment. And it will be such that all men shall remember it and shall call it *The Judgement of Cynwas*."

He turned toward the tribesmen holding horses ready for the pursuit and led the way from that still hall.

9

The Gorse-Grown Hollow

THEY GALLOPED AWAY, swinging beneath leaning boughs, fording streams with a white scatter of foam, whipping their horses eastward and then north. Cynwas went in the front, riding like a vengeful god, hunched in the saddle, his broad sword at his right hip. The four Romans held the middle place, going knee to knee with no thoughts of rank now, always aware that behind them came the Coritani tribesmen, their javelins across their thighs as they galloped.

Once, as they came fast toward a crumbling wall of old gray stone, Marcus called out to Cynwas, "Slower, man! Slower! You'll have your pony down." But the Celt thumped in his heels even harder and took the wall like a bird, seeming hardly to waver in his traveling, and landing so lightly on the far side that his horse's hooves scarcely disturbed the tall grasses. But Cynwas did not turn in the saddle, either to thank or to mock Marcus. He rode like a man alone in the world, ignorant of friends and enemies alike.

Tigidius grunted as his bony mount worked at the hard ground. He said to Marcus, "Hold your tongue, lad. He'll tire first, then we can talk sense to him."

But half a day passed—through woodland, beside rivers, along bridle paths—and Cynwas did not look back. And when the sun stood above the riders' heads and the country opened out toward the great military road, Marcus said to the centurion, "This is madness. The horses

58

will drop dead beneath us, and we shall be too weary to lift a hand to save the girl or to defend ourselves." He kicked hard at his pony's ribs and drew away from the other Romans. Cynwas heard the thudding of hooves and glanced back, red-faced and furious. "Get back, Roman!" he shouted. But Marcus urged his pony onward until he was almost able to reach forward and touch the cloak of Cynwas as it flared out behind him.

Then suddenly the Celt swung round, his thong-whip hissing like a snake, and struck the tribune full across the face with the heavy lash. The Roman gasped, tasted the salt from his broken lips, then with a cry of anger surged forward until he could grasp at the flailing whip. For a moment he thought of dragging Cynwas out of the saddle. But then his fury died back a little and all he did was to wrench the thong away from him, and riding so close that their leg-bones jolted together painfully he yelled, "If you are so much a fool as not to know friend from enemy, then gallop to your death, and good riddance to you!"

He had meant to veer away to the left where the turf was cropped by sheep and seemed easier going instead of straight on, which led to a shadowy basin grown around with gorse-bushes and straggling thorn. But before the words had left him, Cynwas had leaned across and had him by the belt, drawing him from the saddle. Then Marcus saw with horror that the Celt had slipped his sword from the sheath, and holding it with shortened blade was about to push it at him.

Rolling sideways, he watched the bright iron slide past him only an inch from his body, ripping through the fabric of his padded tunic. He let loose the reins and with both hands took the arm of Cynwas, thrusting it down like a stick to be broken over the knee and shouted, "You madman! If you will not be warned, then suffer!"

He saw the sword fly away to his left, the sudden wide staring of the Celt's eyes, then both ponies were down, rolling over and over into the gorse-grown hollow.

59

Now all thoughts of hurting the Celt went from the Roman's mind. He flung up his hands to cover his head and tumbled down and down, among thistles and daisies and dock, like a rolling ball. He heard the horses falling too, heard their great hooves thudding and scraping at the turf, heard the riders behind him shouting and slithering over the edge.

A fleck of foam from one of the horses flew gently through the air and landed on the tribune's cheek. In all that fierce falling he knew what it was, and even put his fingers to it to wipe it away.

And then everything changed. He was no longer angry with Cynwas; no longer afraid that the horses would roll on him, or that the riders behind him would gallop onto him. For now, all at once, he lay among the dead, and what they looked like took his thoughts away from all other things.

At the dry base of the little round basin, where the ground ivy twined about the struggling holly shoots, Novantico lay white-faced and gaping, stripped of his armor, his arms spread wide. And above him and below him, their limbs twisted about bushes, their bodies scratched by wild brambles, lay the other legionaries.

Marcus was on his knees, staring at them, when he realised that Cynwas was beside him, staring also. And halfway down that steep slope the other riders sat aghast at what lay below.

Tigidius spoke first. "I do not see the girl," he said. And then the spell was broken. Marcus and the chieftain rose and stumbled about among the bodies, speechlessly, but now without anger. What had happened to the runaways and their leader drove all fury from the searchers.

Cynwas stood then like a man bewitched, his hand on his head, his blue eyes staring blankly. Marcus came to him and putting his own hand on the Celt's shoulder said, "Someone got to them before we did, brother. Now we must look for Aranrhod."

Cynwas turned and struck at the tribune, catching him at the side of the face with a clenched fist. Marcus hardly moved at the blow, but took the Celt's hand kindly and held it by his chest. He said, "I would have done the same, brother. But now that it has been done, let us forget our fury. Much blood has been shed already. Let us not wait until more runs to waste."

As he said this, a brown-faced tribesman ran up with an arrow in his hand. To Cynwas he said, "Master, they were ambushed by Iceni. These arrow-flights are streaked with blue and red. It is their sign."

Cynwas pushed the man away then turned to Marcus and said, "Do you know what you have done? You have killed my sister, as truly as though you had put the spear to her yourself."

Marcus gazed at him in amazement. "I?" he said. "I killed her?"

Cynwas laughed drily, like a stream dying and said, "She wore your medallion, did she not? They will think she is a Roman brat. At the least she will be a slave for the rest of her poor days."

10

The Long Road

THEY MOUNTED the shuddering ponies once again and quested around like wolves, for a scent. Tigidius said to Marcus, "This is a bad business, lad. But no one can be held to account for it. There are four Romans here to bear witness; you and I will make a formal report when we are able."

Marcus flared out at him. "Witnesses! Reports!" he shouted. "Can you not bring your wooden brain to think of anything else? Do you think that all the world is ruled by witnesses and reports? Do you think all folk are Romans? Is there not room for a little pity in that barrack-block of a world you live in?"

The centurion sat rigid in the saddle while this was said. Then he bowed his head stiffly between his shoulders and said quietly, "The fault is mine, tribune. I spoke as the legion trained me. I ask your pardon. I can say no more."

He said this simply and with no expression in his voice. Marcus looked at him in astonishment, then suddenly realised that this man was old enough to be his father, though they had always gone side by side like youths in friendship. He realised that Tigidius had been his own father's most trusted officer. He turned his pony toward the man and put out his hand. "It is I who should ask pardon," he said. "I spoke ahead of my reason, friend. I am sorry."

The centurion looked him in the eye steadily and without feeling. "The fault is mine, tribune," he repeated. "When we get back to the Colonia, please put on record that I have said those words, sir."

He glanced sideways at the two legionaries as he spoke and they smiled in understanding. Marcus began to pull his pony round and wave his hand to explain himself, but just then Cynwas came beside him and said, "My best tracker has scented the way the killers took. He has a fine nose, and these Iceni go in bare feet. Come, it is to the east. They must be gathering on the Long Road. Come."

They all turned, and gaining the lip of the slope, swung their mounts away to the right, toward the wolds that wallowed like gentle green dolphins with the tall sky over them, blue and empty.

Cynwas spoke only once as they galloped. He said,

"When we come up with the Iceni I shall teach them a stern lesson, tribune. If my sister is unharmed, I shall take off their right hands—no more. If she has been misused, then I shall turn them on spits over a charcoal fire. And you, tribune, shall have the honor of lighting that fire."

Marcus answered, "I have a sister of my own. If this happened to her I should go to law and have the magistrates put the appropriate sentence on the ill-doers. But I should not make myself a worse man than they are by going back a hundred years to gain my vengeance. We Romans did not march halfway across the world to teach you hand-chopping and charcoal fires, Cynwas."

The young chieftain laughed with scorn into the blue air. "Before you came we did well enough, invader. In those days a child could wander in the woods unmolested. All she had to watch for were four-footed wild beasts and little snakes. Now, since you have civilised us, as you say, the beasts have two legs and wear helmets and ride on horses. Rome has given us a great benefit, a great education. I tell you, when we come up with them . . ."

He did not finish the sentence. Instead, as they topped a green rise, they saw—below them and almost half a mile away—a strange thing happening along the straight military road and in the green meadows on either side of it. There was a great confusion of horsemen and footmen, all milling round like fallen leaves in a whirlpool—and many of them, both men and horse, had fallen and were littering the road and fields.

Tigidius cried out, "Tribune, it is the ninth legion. I can see the eagle and the cohort flags. It is my own cohort, but most of them are mounted. There are three tribunes with them on white horses; men you know."

Marcus said drily, "Petillius Cerialis is at their head. I can see as far as you can, friend. I can see his gold helmet with the red plume from here. The legate is laying about him."

As he spoke, the two legionaries who rode behind the party suddenly yelled out, "The ninth! The ninth! Up the ninth!" and galloped forward, kicking their horses' flanks like madmen. Cynwas watched them go, thudding the turf and scattering sheep on either side of them. And when they had gone twenty yards, he turned and nodded to a long-faced man who sat hunched behind him. "Now, Glappi," he said. The man nodded and almost lazily swung his yew-bow from his back and fitted arrows to it. All at once the Romans lay sprawling among the sheep while their puzzled ponies cantered on, then turned and came back to the main party.

Marcus stared at the Celt in fury. "Who gave you orders to do that?" he said. "You have broken the law, you savage. They are my men; not yours to do with as you please."

Cynwas looked back at him with a hard face. He said, "No one gives me orders in my country," he said. "It is they who broke the law—my law. And as for being your men, they were no one's men, being traitors. If you now want to speak the Roman law to them, you are welcome."

Tigidius rode over to the legionaries and dismounting, turned them over. Then he rose and shook his head before returning.

Glappi the long-faced bowman got off his pony smiling, then ran over to the fallen soldiers and carefully withdrew his arrows from them, so as not to bend the slender shafts.

Cynwas leaned down to him as he came back and said, "Not bad, not bad, old one. They were more difficult targets than a roe-deer, but you brought them down within a count of five fingers. Remind me to reward you when we get back with my sister."

Marcus was so angry he could not speak; but the centurion edged his horse beside him and said, "I have made a note of their names, for the records, sir. Both of them come from Heracles so you will not have letters to write home to their families. They were runaway slaves, and have none."

Marcus had regained his breath now and turned towards Cynwas, but the Celt put up his hand and silenced him. "Pay attention to what goes on below you, soldier," he said. "What has happened to these two is happening to all your cohort. See, they are falling everywhere; and now their leader, the little man in the gold helmet, is turning and leading them away northward, back up your fine road! I must say, you Romans make fine riders—when the enemy is at your tail."

The centurion gasped, "Oh no, oh no! Look, sir, they have given ground. My cohort is retreating."

Cynwas said calmly, "Soon you will have no cohort, friend. Those Iceni down there run like the wind and cast their spears as truly as Marru, the god of death. If five of them get to your Lindum to shriek at the gates for them to open, then they will be lucky men and should go home and turn their hands to farming straightway— before an arrow takes them."

Tigidius rode forward, his hard face set in an expression of quiet anger. He said, "Do not jeer too quickly, Briton. The ninth legion never leaves a setback unavenged. There are other cohorts, almost as good as my own. They will come out of the gates you scoff at, and then these Iceni will mourn for their dead, mourn for their tribe, and mourn for their lost past the rest of their lives— those who are left to mourn."

Cynwas did not even look at him, but whistled ironically into the morning air like a gay lark.

This angered Marcus more than anything. He said quite loudly, "You seem to have forgotten one thing, horse-thief. Your sister whom you profess to love is down there among the savages. No doubt they will be doing to her what they are doing to my fellow-Romans since, as you have said, they will think she is of my people."

Now Cynwas stopped whistling and gazed down, his

65

face changed as though a cold hand had passed over it. "Come," he said, "there are wagons among them. She will surely be there, among the women of the tribe."

He galloped off without any more words and the others had hard business to keep up with him.

Here and there the moorland had been broken into by the plowshare, and the upturned clods of earth flew back under the horses' hooves into the faces of the riders behind. Then, in other places, stones and even boulders had been dragged out of the ground to make square sheep-pens, sometimes with walls running beside them to keep out wolves. The Celts were lazy builders, but even so they had set up waist-high barriers of dry-stone and most riders would have reined their horses around these walls. But not Cynwas; he galloped over them or crashed through them, sometimes coming close to bringing his pony down. It was like riding behind a madman. Once Marcus called out to him, "Pull in, you fool, or you'll have us all down."

But Cynwas went on silently, like a gray ghost riding through a black dream. He did not ride in the world of men now, but in the world of vengeance. His eyes were blind to walls and his ears deaf to words. He went like an earth-skimming hawk after its quarry, daft to all reason.

Then at last they went into a low green valley where sheep were grazing and a narrow stream wound about among the stones. The far side was a steep one and even Cynwas had to give his mount a breathing-space now.

So they were long enough in topping the rise, and when they could see the road again most of the armies had gone, leaving only the wagons and the folk who looked after them. And the dead.

II

Among the Wagons

MARCUS DREW in his breath with fury. Legionaries lay everywhere among the coarse grass, most of them stripped of their war-gear and even their rough leather undershirts. The wounds they bore were not pleasant to look at. Even Tigidius, who had seen most things that sword or spear could do in his long service under the eagles, turned his head away from the piled bodies.

To Marcus he said, "This is not war. This is butchery. There is no honor here."

Cynwas turned on him and said, "No, Roman—it is only honorable when you wolves do it. If the hounds bite back at you, you howl."

Then they came upon the wagons—long carts of clumsy oak, piled high with war-stuff and Roman armor. In a little square, with these carts about them like a stockade, a group of women danced in a circle, chanting, their faces streaked with warpaint; some of them were even wearing Roman helmets or carrying Roman shields in mockery. They were singing in their own language, an ancient and monotonous song that rose and fell only a few notes, and to which it was terrible to listen. It was more like the vicious buzzing of hornets than a sound that could come from human throats.

Cynwas said in a chill voice, "You are hearing their victory chant, tribune. It was ancient before the wolf suckled your ancestors, Romulus and Remus. It was ancient before those Greek fools fought at Troy. Do you like the sounds you hear, my friend?"

Marcus set his jaw and sat upright on his borrowed pony. He said coldly, "Can you see your sister?"

Then Cynwas rode among the Icenian women and said to the eldest, who wore a wreath of holly around her head, "I am the chief here. I am Cynwas and my heart is set against Rome. These Romans who ride with me are my hostages. I seek my sister, Aranrhod. Where shall I find her?"

The woman in the laurel wreath stared up at him blankly, as though he came from another dream and said, "You are of the Coritani. You are not of our folk. You are like Romans to us, man We only know you as horse-thieves, man. We have our dancing to do. Seek your sister in some other place. Turn over the dead for her. If she is small, she may lie under her Roman friends. Do not trouble us, we have our dance to do. Such victory does not come to us often."

Then she turned away from him and the women began to take up the step again, on the wide and dusty road, with the dead soldiers all about them.

Cynwas glared in such fury that his eyes almost started out. He leaned from his shaggy pony and took hold of the woman's shift at the shoulder, drawing her toward him.

"What are you?" he shouted. "Are you savages? I ask for my kinswoman and you treat me like a stranger, like a Roman. Is there no pride among the Iceni now that their master, Prasutagus, has gone?"

It was a terrible moment. The woman glared up at him and raised her right forefinger toward his forehead. Marcus saw Cynwas stiffen on his pony and seem to draw himself in and become small, as though awaiting a blow. The women in the dancing-ring all stood stiff and silent, leaning forward, their white-painted faces with the deep

68

blue streaks across cheek and forehead like the faces of witches, half-smiling, half-grim.

Then from the tallest wagon,—one painted in black— a voice came out over their heads, hoarse and commanding. It said: "Leave them be, priestess. They are not for your hand but for mine. Have no fear. They will be seen to. They will come to learn."

Marcus swung around and saw who spoke. It was a woman he had seen once before, riding down a narrow lane toward the great stones. Then she had been like a warrior, lithe in her shirt and as glorious as a battle-youth. Now, she was heavier in build, and her hair carried streaks of badger-gray in it. Her face had lost its fineness. Over the white ochre, the blue streaks gave it the look of painted stone. There was no mercy in that face.

Marcus leaned toward the centurion and whispered, "It is the queen. It is their Boadicea, the Victory-Queen. For the love of Mithras, stay silent now. Keep your tongue on the rein, Tigidius."

The centurion nodded and looked down at his horse's neck.

Cynwas was the first to speak. With some pride he said, "Lady, I ask no favors. I am a Celt, like you. I seek only my sister."

There was another terrible silence. Then the voice from the cart said stiffly, "You ask no favors, yet you ask for your sister? What sort of talk is that, O Brother to Romans? Have you already learned to reason like them— to push favors aside with the right hand, then to take them with the left?"

As the queen spoke, she switched her fur-clad shoulders with a horsetail fly whisk. Her shaggy russet hair streaked with gray flared about her as the whisk caught it at times, half-covering her lined face. The robes she now wore were stained with mud and dust, and tattered

69

at the hem. She wore no shoes upon her feet and Marcus saw that her toes and ankles were scarred and begrimed, as though she had marched with her warriors along the road toward Lindum until the battle had started.

He said, bowing his head in a movement of respect, "Lady, it is the duty of the conqueror to show mercy and humility. My people lie about among the grasses, having felt the power of your arm. My commander has been put to flight with such dishonor that it will need many victories to let him hold up his head again. What has been done is over and finished. You have humbled us, lady. You have given us a wound from which it will take years to recover. But this man beside me is another matter. He is not a Roman. He does not deserve your anger. He seeks only a harmless child, who is his sister. Show yourself great in victory, lady, and whatever you do to us Romans, help him in his search. You have daughters of your own and must know the love and tenderness that folk in a family bear to one another."

He had hardly finished speaking when the horsetail slashed across his face, half-blinding him. Tears ran down his cheeks but he did not raise his hand to wipe them away. Instead, he forced his lips to form themselves into a smile, as though the queen had greeted him like an old friend. Then the horsetail struck savagely again, and this time the force of the blow was so great that Marcus had to lower his head and blink his eyes.

Boadicea stared hard at him, her own lips now set in a terrible smile. As he looked up at last, she said in a deep whisper, "In all these years you have learned little, Roman, although you have grown tall on our British food and drink. You are still that headstrong boy who sat on the horse before me, blocking my way along the road. Only now you have more words rolling about on your tongue."

Marcus felt a shudder go down his back and the hairs on his neck stiffen; that this woman should have remembered him so clearly after such a long while! "Lady," he said, "when we met before, you gave me a brooch and promised that if our paths crossed again I should have the right to use your road. I do not ask for that privilege on my own account, but for Cynwas of the Coritani. Give him leave to pass among your people and to find his sister."

Then Boadicea looked over his head far away toward Lindum, as though she were seeing into the distant past, and for a moment her stiff painted face seemed to soften a little. Quietly she said, "Do you still carry the brooch I gave you, Roman? Do you still treasure it?"

Marcus smiled up at her and nodded. "I still carry it, lady," he answered. "It is in my pouch now. Would you care to see it?"

She did not answer him for a time, but seemed to go off into a dream. Flies buzzed about the horses' tails, hooves stamped impatiently in the dust of the road, and the women dancers began to sway slowly like reeds in the wind, as though they were tired of it all and wished to start their low-pitched chanting again.

Then Boadicea closed her blue-painted eyelids and said in a strange whisper, "And do you trust the promise I gave you with that brooch so many years ago, Roman? Do you still believe the words I spoke when you were a boy, and I, little more than a girl?"

Marcus sat upright on his horse. He said, "Yes, lady, I still trust your promise."

The shock of the third blow almost toppled him to the ground. This time it was the wooden handle of the whisk that struck him, not the horsehair. He heard the queen's voice cry out, "Then, the more fool you!" And as he staggered, pulling his mount round to keep from falling, he heard the screech of a bone whistle, and Boadicea's voice almost screaming, "Into the wagon with these fools! They will make an evening's entertainment for us when the ale-cup passes round."

Marcus heard the swift pattering of bare feet toward him. Hard hands took him by the arms and legs, then suddenly he was down in the dust, held there cruelly by the dancers with the war-streaked faces. He saw Tigidius rein back his pony, so that it reared high above the clustered women, but his freedom only lasted a moment; then he too was down, face to the road, and powerless. Cynwas saw this, then, giving a high shout, swung his mount away and kicked hard at its sides. It seemed that he would break free, along the road that swung southward among the overhanging boughs. But he had scarcely gone ten paces when a tall man, dressed in wolfskins, started up from the ditch and flung a heavy stone hammer at him. It caught him hard below the right arm and seemed to sweep him from the pony's back, as a man's hand can sweep away a troublesome fly.

The frightened pony galloped on without him and disappeared among the dark green trees. The man in the wolfskins went over to the Briton and picked him up, as though he were a harvest-doll of straw. Then, striding to the wagon, he flung Cynwas down before the queen.

She did not speak to the warrior and when he had backed away, she turned to the women and said, "Bind them with wet hide at wrist and ankle. I want them to know what being a captive really means. I want them to know, in their bodies, what I have suffered in my heart during these months."

And when this was done, the captives were thrown into the back of the great wagon like bundles of bracken meant for the fires.

Tigidius screwed up his face in wry humor and said, "Well, I have been in some positions, tribune, but never one like this."

Cynwas opened his eyes painfully now and said, "Before the day is out, you will look back on this as comfort. She has learned her trade well, Roman. Your own butchers have taught her something."

Then the wagon began to turn and rumbled down the road and Cynwas began to groan from the pain of his hurt ribs.

12

Going South

THE NEXT DAYS were agony for the prisoners in the black wagon. As they rolled on southward along the Ermine Street, men and women from the many tribes on either side came in to join the Iceni, and all of them wanted to see the Romans and to taunt them and strike at them. Tigidius said grimly, "I think they are taking us to Camulodunum for some reason or other best known to themselves. But if we get halfway there without having our skulls cracked, I shall be surprised."

Marcus nodded. "At least we are still alive," he said. "And that is more than can be said for half of our legion. I never thought I would see the ninth so mauled. It is like the end of the world. My father would have fallen on his sword if he had led his men into such an ambush."

Cynwas was now feeling better than he had, although the Iceni had not treated his wounded side. He leaned forward and smiling bitterly, said, "Now we all have something to mourn. I have my sister, and you have your crippled legion. We are both in the same boat. I am sorry I quarreled with you. Can we be friends again?"

The tribune gazed at him emptily for a while, then

smiled and said, "Cynwas, you old fool! Of course we are friends. But I will tell you this; if we are both alive when this affair is over, I shall take you behind the fortress gates somewhere and give you the biggest thrashing you ever had, with bare fists, just to show you how much I like you—and also to knock some sense into your thick British head. Is that a bargain?"

Cynwas nodded. "As long as we get Aranrhod back I will agree to anything," he said, "Though don't expect me to fight fairly, as you call it. I shall use my feet as well. I am not one of these Greek fist-fighters."

Then Tigidius broke in, staring over the side of the wagon. "Look at the fields," he said. "They are trampled flat. No grain has been sown down here. What will the tribes feed on this year?"

Marcus looked across the rolling wilderness of dust and burned trees. He said, "This can mean only one thing. If the tribes have not planted their fields, it is because they hope to eat elsewhere. You are as good at guessing as I am, centurion."

Tigidius said slowly, "There are Roman grain supplies and cattle at Camulodunum, but they are mainly for the veterans who have retired to live out their days there."

Marcus said grimly, "Guess again, friend."

The centurion said, "Do you mean Verulamium? That is off the track, isn't it?"

Marcus said, "I do mean Verulamium, and it is not off the track if you consider how this revolt is spreading. If you listen to the folk about us you will hear that there are Catuvellauni, and even Atrebates, marching beside the wagons."

They listened for a time. Then Tigidius said suddenly, "By Mithras, but the Atrebates come from south of Londinium. Can it have spread so far?"

Marcus lowered his head. "I think they mean to take the supply base at Londinium itself. If they do, then Rome is finished here. The legions will starve. What can they do to help themselves? Suetonius is at the other side of the province with the fourteenth and twentieth legions. They have their hands full dealing with the Ordovices. The second legion, at Glevum, is pinned down by the Silures and daren't take their eyes off the hills for an hour. They depend on being supplied from Londinium. If the Iceni take that base, the legions will starve."

Tigidius said shortly, "Once hunger begins to grip them, Marcus, they will move. You can depend on that. They will cross the country to see what has happened to their food rations. They are soldiers."

The tribune laughed emptily. "They would need to be more than soldiers," he said. "They would need to be birds, and big birds at that—eagles, you could say—to cross the woodland and mountains so as to reach Londinium before the Iceni could. They have over two hundred miles to march, while the tribes have less than half that distance—and a good road that we have built them to travel down."

Cynwas yawned and said, "You Romans—always supply bases, roads, marching! You consider life as though it was a matter of measuring everything. But you forget one important thing."

Marcus said, "Go on, tell us—I am sure you mean to in any case. So get it over."

Cynwas said calmly, "You forget that the tribes do not measure everything. For them, distance and time mean nothing. If they find a place they like they will stay there until they are tired of it."

Tigidius said, "Or until they have burned it to the ground and cannot live there any longer because of the stench of charred houses and dead bodies."

Cynwas shrugged his shoulders. "You may put it in the Roman way if you wish, centurion," he said. "But, I tell you, this habit of the tribes might be your only salvation. I do not say that you deserve it after what was done at Venta Icenorum, but it could happen that the legions reach Londinium in time—if only the Iceni delay a little while at Camulodunum, eating up the veterans' corn and breaking down those fine houses and temples and theaters that you folk took so much trouble to set up there."

Marcus shut his eyes. His lips moved in a prayer, but those in the wagon beside him could not hear what he was saying, or to which god he addressed his words.

13

The White Garlands

ON THE FOURTH DAY of their journey, the tall tribesman in a coat of wolfskins climbed into the wagon and cut their leg-thongs. He smiled as he did this, his blue-streaked face twisting savagely. When they looked up at him he said, "Out! Walk like the others. Why should you ride?"

Cynwas said, "The queen, where is she? We have not seen her for days."

The man raised his eyebrows. "Are you so glad to see her?" he asked. "You should be happy not to see her. She has gone riding among other tribes to raise them. When she comes back she will have you dropped from a tree onto pointed stakes set in the ground. I tell you this so that you will look forward to her return."

Then he jumped from the black wagon and laughed

as he went up the line to other wagons with his bronze knife.

Cynwas said, "He is not jesting. He speaks the truth. It is one of their customs."

For a mile they did not speak again, but stumbled on along the dusty road among the tribesmen, being jostled and prodded with lance points. Sometimes women and even children pushed up to them and struck them across the face with sticks or thong-whips. But it was all done light-heartedly and with laughter, as though the Iceni now bore them little ill-will. Once a party of young girls brought garlands of white flowers and set them on the heads of the prisoners, singing as they did so. Now the two Romans had lost all their armor and, like Cynwas, shuffled barefooted, dressed only in their ragged shirts.

And once an old woman with a clay pot in her hand reached out and daubed their faces with blue dye as she passed them. Marcus said, "I think they have elected us to their tribe. In this war paint and wearing this garland, I almost feel like one of them."

Cynwas said in a hoarse voice, "They put garlands on the necks of their cattle and daub them with paint before they sacrifice them, tribune. They think that the gods will only accept those who go happily to their death."

Tigidius snorted and flung off his garland then; but a warrior ran forward and put it back on the centurion's head roughly and thumped him hard in the back with a spear-shaft. Tigidius said, "Well, that is one lesson I have learned. They are a civil folk, these Iceni."

By midday they passed through a burned out village where the reed huts still smouldered. Cattle lay dead in the compound; their hooves stuck up in the air and swarms of black flies buzzed over them. Near to the roadside was a small house built of stone, but now so toppled and blackened by fire that it was hard to believe a Roman had built it. In the small courtyard three folk lay stretched out—a woman and a small boy with yellow hair, and a few paces from them a dark-haired man still wearing a legionary's breastplate. Between them lay a smashed keg from which oysters were scattered across the tiles.

Marcus said, "It must have come on them quickly. That is the one consolation."

Tigidius looked beyond that stark little place and whispered in camp Latin, "At least they had a little time together, the Roman and his British wife. They are beyond our pity now. Think to the future. Look, four hundred paces down the road there is a stretch of woodland that comes right to the road-edge. If we broke away from this column, we might get among the trees and be away, with luck."

Cynwas heard him and said, "There would be others waiting for us when the wood ended. And these Iceni can run like stags. We should die within half a mile."

Marcus frowned. "At least we should know the worst then," he said. "That would be better than waiting for the other thing we have been promised."

But Cynwas shook his head. "If I go with you, I shall never find my sister," he whispered. "At least if I stay with them, I might see her again before I die. I might be able to beg mercy for her. I cannot go with you."

Marcus looked back up the long road. It was black with folk as far as the eye could see. The dust that rose from their shuffling feet threw up a haze, and above that haze black birds flew squawking, following the great column. He thought that half Britain must be on the move. It came to him that if, by some jest of the gods, he could get away from this sickening army, he might even be given the luck to press on to Londinium and warn the garrison there. It was a small chance, but suddenly he knew that it was his duty to take it. He thought sadly that this was what his father would have done; so he leaned sideways and took the hand of Cynwas and gripped it hard. "Stay, brother," he said. "This is your place. May Mithras smile down on you and the little sister."

Then, singing and laughing like the tribesmen about him, he began to push toward the side of the road, slapping shoulders and jostling like anybody else. The warriors slapped in return but did not stop him from edging away. Out of the corner of his eye he saw that Tigidius was beside him, shouting out and joking in very poor Celtic. The centurion had never learned more than a few words of the language, but he bawled them out as though he were on the parade ground at Lindum again, training auxiliaries.

Marcus half-turned once and said in a low voice, "Don't try to do too much, old one. A little is enough with a voice like yours. We do not want them to notice us too much."

But the tribesmen did not seem to be thinking of their prisoners now. They were singing a strange song in a deep droning tone, about a god who was shut inside an oak tree and called out to be fed with blue-eyed children. The Iceni were a dark-eyed folk in the main and Marcus shuddered to hear this old enmity coming out. He wondered what color Aranrhod's eyes were. He had forgotten in view of all the things that had happened since he last saw the little girl. Then, by some queer shift of the mind he suddenly pictured his own sister Livia, with her funny light-colored eyes, and her little baby girl, Drusilla. Had Drusilla got blue eyes, he wondered?

Then Tigidius tapped him on the arm and said quite stiffly, "Watch out, sir. The wood is coming up. We should get ready to go within five paces."

Marcus felt his heart leap up. He felt the old twitching of his fingers and toes. The tribesmen were all in a lost dream with their savage song. On the slope toward the left of the road a score of Icenian boys had run out, swinging bone bull-roarers that buzzed like gigantic bees in time to the song. Before them pranced an old man wearing a stag's mask, the stiff face grinning, the long antlers nodding, the teeth all yellow, sticking out from the drawn-back leather. Marcus noticed, almost without any disgust, that the old man swung two heads by their brown hair, knocking them together to keep time to the dance.

Then he saw the first of the trees coming beside him and said, "Now!"

He plunged to his right, sensed that the centurion was with him, felt that he had knocked a man down, then a woman, and with the coarse grasses up to his waist, he was free.

He felt a slight thud on his left shoulder but kept running. Dimly behind him he heard Tigidius shout, "Pull it out, you fool. Pull it out."

He did not look around, but felt with his right hand toward his shoulder and grasped the arrow. It had not gone in far, but it was quite sharp as the barbed flint head came clear again.

He called out, "That wouldn't have knocked a hare down, friend. We can still teach them something, old lad!"

Then he began to feel rather sick, but his heart was galloping like a front-line courser now and his legs wouldn't stop. He saw trees slanting to left and right of him, as though they were being thrown at him. He wondered who was throwing them, and laughed. He suddenly remembered that he was very hungry. He thought that a runner must need good food to keep running.

In a way he wished his father could see him now, running among the oaks with half Britain howling for his blood.

Then all at once he heard a great silence. He heard that the Iceni were not howling at all. Even the bull-roarers had stopped. And at the same time he was aware that the thudding footsteps of Tigidius had stopped also. Marcus wondered if he had died from the arrow. He had listened to many old soldiers from Germany and Palestine, who had described what it was like to die. Of course, they had not died; but they had seen many of their friends in that state and had told how men seemed to go off. Some of them went very quietly, as though they were leaving the feast-board after a good meal; others were still in the middle of their howling when they grew still and let their heads bump on the earth.

Marcus ran through a low thorn-bush just then and the thorns hurt him far more than the arrow did, so he knew that he was alive. Indeed, he almost stopped to rub his shins.

But he didn't stop then. He went on another ten paces before he stopped. And when he did there was no doubt about it; he had to stop. No one, not even Hercules, could have gone on.

And a voice that he knew almost better than any voice was calling out to him, "How pretty you look, tribune, in that white garland. Yes, how comely. They did not tell me you Romans wore such things. And that blue war paint! What war are you going to, my friend, in such a hurry?"

14

The Queen on the Cart

IN a broad glade, under the oversweeping boughs, Queen Boadicea sat staring before her at the running Romans. Behind her in the woodland, yawning and laughing, leaning on their long spears, waited five hundred tribesmen. Some of them were Silures from the distant west, wearing their catskin bonnets and their eagle plumes.

Seated high on a war-cart, pulling in the reins Boadicea said, "What war are you going to in such great haste?"

Marcus stopped then, a man coming out of a dream. He saw Tigidius beside him, bending double and coughing, suddenly grown old. He said in a vacant voice, "A man runs, woman. Sometimes he runs toward victory, sometimes toward gold; sometimes toward the sun, the dawn, toward freedom, or toward nothing. He runs. That is why they call him a man, because he moves through life and does not lie down and die like a beaten animal."

She was sitting on a heap of Roman gear; helmets and cuirasses and shields. She settled herself then and flung some of them over the side of the war-cart. She said, smiling thinly, "Today, in this green oak grove, I am the goddess in the cart. I am Nerthus of the dark woodland. I am that She of the German-tribes, the Kindred of the Forests. Are you not ashamed to speak of what a man is to me, when you see before you the greatest of women?"

Marcus sat down upon the grass and put his head between his knees, the way soldiers are taught when they feel faint from marching. He felt her power coming down over his neck and back so he sat up again and tried to smile, as though he had not felt it at all. He said to Tigidius, "Did you hear someone addressing us, centurion?"

But Tigidius did not answer, and when Marcus looked again she was still there, her face stiff under its ochre mask, her hair all starry and staring like the rays of the sun with its yellow clay dressing. But most of all that made him wonder was the great eye painted in the middle of her forehead, as though it glowed and pulsed at him. He put his hand across his own eyes to avoid it, for it seemed to send off sparks of fire that went into his head. He said, his eyes covered, "I only know that there is a beast abroad now; that good men have died for nothing, and children too."

The cold voice came back at him again: "All men die, Roman. And in a land that knows old Nero's rule children are fortunate if they see light, much less grow old enough to play one game of hunting through their fathers' woods."

Marcus got up and yawned like the dark-skinned tribesmen. He tried to stretch his arms, but suddenly found that the pain in his shoulder was more than he had thought. So he dropped his arms and slapped his right thigh with his good hand and said, "It cannot be done, woman. You are trying to do what cannot be done. Look, let me explain to you: there is only one world, and over that world there is only one master—Rome. Yes, yes, I understand, you bridle at that; but it is true. We all have something to bridle at—I have my sore shoulder and a dead father at this time. You have a dead husband and a grievance against Decianus Catus, that dolt of a procurator who broke open your family-chests and took the treasures. But it is true. I tell you, it is . . ."

He was so taken up by his own tired words that he did not see the queen's frown, or her signal to the dark runners behind the cart. But he felt their hands on him, and felt their hard feet kicking into his face as they swung him onto a pole like a caught bear. Once as they carried him along, he glanced sideways and saw that Tigidius was on a pole as well. This puzzled him, because poor Tigidius had not even opened his mouth to speak to this strange, savage queen.

Then a man who walked beside the pole with a polished flint axe in his hand, bent over gently and said, "Sleep well, youth. If you were my son I would be proud of you. What a shame you are a Roman."

Then the man did something and Marcus went flying among the gold and silver stars.

And when the stars had come to rest again and the dark blue heavens had lightened to a misty gray, he opened his eyes and looked about him.

He was still in the depths of the forest, with the boughs so woven over his head that they seemed like a thatched roof. On the ground, among the dried grasses and the ferns, fires burned. It was night and owls called from away in the trees, hunting for other things than Romans.

He was sitting against a fallen oak-bole and Tigidius was beside him to the right running his tongue round his lips, as though he marched in Libya under the sun there. Marcus looked again and saw that now Cynwas was with them again, bound as they were and sitting on his left.

The old man wearing the stag-mask and the antlers sat before them, beyond the wood fire, muttering to himself and touching a skin drum with tired fingers.

Marcus called out, "Hey, old man, where is the waterskin? My lips are cracking. Where is the waterskin?"

He had to say it many times, and when the old man noticed him Marcus saw that the eyes which glared from the stiff mask were as blind as flint.

Tigidius said painfully to Marcus, "I have tried a score of times while you were asleep. He is not in this world, that old man. His heart is in the drums and in what they say—whatever that may be. I do not understand the tongue his fingers talk on the skins. But we shall get nothing from him, I can tell you."

Marcus shook his head to clear it, then said, "I would like a cup of clear, cold water, friend. How strange life is when a man wants no more than that!"

The centurion looked away. He said softly, "I do not think we shall have even that much before they impale us. I cannot see an army on the march wasting water. Frankly, if I were in command I would not use good water on such as we are."

Marcus said, "That is because you are a soldier, and only a soldier, old one. But these are woodland tribes and field tribes. They are not true fighting-men. It is worth another try."

But before he could call to the antler man again, Cynwas came awake and said to him, "Be quiet, you fool. I have heard that they have my sister here with them. Please do nothing to make them angrier than they are. I beg you."

Marcus turned round painfully in his thongs and looked at Cynwas. He was hardly the man that he had known before. He had been cruelly treated by the Iceni when his friends had made their forlorn run through the woods.

Marcus bowed his head. "I beg your pardon, brother," he said. "I will be quiet. Why, we will drink a barrel of water later on, when this is over."

He laughed, but Cynwas did not join him. Nor did the centurion, who found that he had lost two teeth on the right side from the kicks he had taken in that pole-ride through the forest.

15

Under the Oak Boughs

THERE was a sudden stirring throughout the woodland, as though all the trees were sighing and groaning and shifting their deep roots to gather as a great army, and to come to a meeting before battle. Or as though all the creatures—the foxes and wolves, the deer, the sullen bears, the wild dogs, the sly lynx—were on the move, seeking pasture or berries or prey.

Marcus felt the hair standing up on his neck. His eyes

darted to left and right, and at first he saw nothing in the dimness of the thickly-columned woodland. Then, like the figures in some horrible vision, lit by torches, he saw what was coming into the trodden glade where he and the others lay bound.

Men in the stiff-painted leather masks of hawks and eagles, their feathered cloaks floating behind them came first, flapping their wings and shrieking out, as though they poised for the steep. Then came devil-dancers, their thin bodies daubed with white clay, their faces hidden by long shield-like masks of dark wood. Behind them swayed forty young men, dressed as for war, swinging bone bull-roarers in a surge that pained the ears. They came on like men in a trance. Then came the young girls, their long hair white with ashes, their faces blackened with soot, their eyes ringed round with blood-red. Each one carried a skull in her left hand and a short spear in her right; and with every step each one beat on the skull with the spear-blade, as though on a drum, setting up a ghastly clacking counter-beat to the bull-roarers.

Tigidius said grimly to the tribune, "For this we Romans have wasted our lives over a hundred years. Only for this."

Marcus drew in a deep breath, the pain of his arm stabbing at him again and said, "They have gone back to the childhood of their people. They have forgotten all we have tried to teach them. If anyone is to blame it would be two fat men—called Decianus Catus and Nero. Now we are reaping the crop they sowed, and the bread it makes needs some chewing."

Cynwas was sitting with his head bowed and his eyes shut. His shoulders and legs were shuddering. His lips were moving all the time, like those of a man praying to be guarded against evil spirits.

Then all at once Marcus saw what came next, and turned toward the Celt and said, "Look, brother. Look!"

Cynwas raised his head and opened his eyes. Less than

86

a hundred paces away, well lit by torches, six young men dressed in green cloth and wearing headgear made of oak and alder and ash leaves carried a wattle-hurdle on their shoulders. Sitting on it, her arms and legs bound with thongs, was Aranrhod. Cynwas saw the ash on her head and the black streaks down her face. He saw the white linen shift in which they had dressed her, even the Roman medallion that still hung round her slender neck.

He said, "No! No! Look, Marcus, they have chosen her for the sacrifice! They cannot do it. They cannot do it."

The young girl's face was calm and showed no terror at what lay before her. She too was like someone in a deep sleep. Her eyes were closed and their lids stained a deep blue. Marcus had trouble in recognizing the little girl who had tricked him so gaily in the wood when he had ridden in with his squadron.

He said to Cynwas, "Take courage, brother. They are only trying to make us afraid. She will come out of it."

But he knew that he was like a man who whistles to keep his heart up in the dark. As for Tigidius, he was looking away now, trying to shut the scene from his mind.

Then suddenly all stopped; all the prancing and roaring and clacking, all the wailing and groaning and deep sighing. The forest glade was silent again. And the many dancers seemed to fade to left and right, so as to leave a space along the central aisle for some great one to travel down.

It was the queen on the cart, dressed as they had last seen her, but now surrounded on every side by her counselors, wearing deerhide robes slung over their shoulders like Roman togas.

"Look, Tigidius," Marcus whispered. "They even have wreaths of laurels on their heads. We have taught them something after all, though to see what they make of our teaching is enough to bring tears to the eyes."

The centurion stared before him, but did not answer.

Then the horns began to howl from somewhere deep in that dark forest. And when their howling had grown almost unbearable, they stopped all at once. And Boadicea stood upright in her chariot and called out in a dreamer's voice: "See, we have come at last; and we have brought the offering for the green gods. We have brought the one who will speak our words to Diana the Maiden, when we have set her free of the body that hampers her pleadings now."

Then the bull-roarers started and the white skulls began to clatter. Cynwas dropped his head and tried to shut out the sound.

Boadicea spoke again above the din and called out, "Have you anything to say, Aranrhod the Blessed? Have you a message to leave to kith and kin, my child?"

Now Cynwas looked up, his eyes fixed on the young girl. But Aranrhod did not even open her eyes. She shook her head gently from right to left and then sat as still as an image.

"See," called the queen, "she is ready for the journey. She knows no kith and kin on earth, now that she has been chosen. Light the fires, set the stakes in the earth. Let the young one fare forth while her heart is with Diana."

Now some of the women ran forward, bringing stones to set in a circle, while others flung brushwood and ferns into a great pile in the middle of the stones. Then four counselors brought ash stakes, sharpened at one end, and set them in a ring about the fire.

Tigidius said sharply, "This has gone too far. This is an insult to us all. It cannot be allowed."

Cynwas was still frozen. His lips moved, but no words came from him. Then all at once he turned his head toward Marcus, and the expression on his face was the saddest the Roman had ever seen.

The tribune struggled at his bonds and tried to stand upright, but the tough deerhide dragged him down again.

He shouted out, as though he were back on the parade ground at Lindum, "Stop this, you barbarians. This has gone too far."

A man wearing the eagle-mask with its curved bronze beak ran forward and thrust a short stabbing-spear at the Roman's face. He did not flinch, and before the eagle-dancer could do him harm the queen called out again, "Wait a while, my people. The gallant Roman wishes to speak a prayer over the girl before we send her to the green goddess."

Marcus sat back and tried to stop the shuddering of his limbs. Then in a clear voice, so that all could hear, he said, "Boadicea, Lady of Victories, the prayer I wish to make is to you and not to the green goddess."

The forest glade was suddenly heavy with murmurings, as though some wrong had been done, some mistake made in the ritual. But the queen held up the spear in her right hand and all was quiet again. Then, in a gentler voice, she cried out, "Take the Roman to my bower. Let him speak to me face to face, alone, if he dares. Let him make his prayer in the secret darkness, as a man should."

She turned her cart about and went back among the clustered folk. Then, before he had seen the last of her, Marcus was lifted up bodily and carried away, as roughly as though he were a sack of grain.

They bumped him painfully among the oak boughs, but at last, beyond the light of the torches, he sensed that they were going under some sort of doorway; then down into the darkness. Everything now had a dank scent as though they were in a low cavern.

And suddenly they flung him down onto the hard rock. He felt damp mosses against his face and the chill of water by his feet. And then for a time all was silent, except for the trickling sound that seemed to come down the wall away to his left.

He lay awhile, then said, "Is there anyone here with me?"

And after a space, the queen's voice said softly, "Yes, Marcus. There is one here with you who will be in your mind all your life, however long you live. And that might be one hour, or fifty years."

He said, "Why are we in the darkness, lady? Do you fear to face Rome?"

He heard her laugh about three paces away from him. Then she answered, "I am beyond fear, Marcus. Consider what has happened to my family—I have no more to lose. Then consider what is to happen to those who stand against my great army. I have all to gain. So, I do not fear."

He said again, "Why are we in the darkness, my lady?"

Her voice was even gentler than before. She said, "I am pleased that you still call me 'my Lady.' You have not forgotten the little lesson I taught you in that sunken lane when you were a child. And Rome will not forget the lesson I shall teach her now, and Rome is not a child."

Marcus sighed with weariness and said for the third time, "*Why* are we in the darkness, woman?"

This time Boadicea answered almost before the question was asked. She said, "Because I do not wish to hurt your pride, tribune. That is all. In the darkness, words can be said that would not come to the lips in the light. You are a proud young man, just as you were a proud boy. Ah, I saw it even then, and I would have loved to have taken you to be my youngest brother at that time! . . ." She paused awhile, then went on quickly, "Look, tribune, I am speaking to you in confidence now, as great ones should. My folk are simple field-diggers and herdsmen. They cannot understand what great ones must suffer. For them all is black or white, winter or summer, pain or joy. But we who rule others know that life is not so simple, yet we have to make it seem so to their weak wits."

Marcus groaned as the damp took hold of his wounded shoulder. The queen said, "We must see to that arrow

90

wound. The flint barbs that the older tribes use are not clean. They are dipped in unclean things, and so, however shallow the wound, bring sickness."

He said quite firmly, "We are not here to talk of arrow wounds, lady. Say what is in your mind."

After he had spoken, he felt almost afraid to have raised his voice against this queen.

But her own voice came back as calmly as before. She said, "Marcus, all has its season—crops, fruit-trees, empires. Every man's life has its time of growth, of fullness, of decay. Rome is dying fast, dying on her feet like a drought-starved old cow. This has become plain to me in the last weeks. Once I had the courage to move out from Venta your legions could not stop me, yet for years we have thought they could stop the sun from crossing the sky if they wished! It is strange! The great ninth legion, your own legion, has run screaming back into its kennel with half its men stark. The second sits shivering at Glevum, under the coward Poenius Postumus, afraid to move an inch outside the camp walls. The fourteenth and twentieth are stuck in Mona, or in the hills of the west among savages, and could not get across the land to me even if they had eagles' wings!"

Marcus said drily, "Suetonius could make them cover a hundred miles in three days, lady. And in a week, they could be tearing at your throat. They would show no mercy, lady. Of that you can take my word."

He sensed that she had come closer to him. He even thought he felt the little draught of air as her skirt brushed by him. She said, above him now, "In a week, my tribune, I shall have done all my work. They would come back to a desert land. They would come back only to drag their weary, starving bodies down to the shore to look for ships. But, my young counselor, there would be no ships. We should have burned them all. Then how would your brave fourteenth and twentieth go on, with no ships? Would they swim across to Gaul or Germany?

91

Or would your fat emperor fly out on his gilded wings and waft them across the seas to safety?"

Marcus thought awhile, then said, "At the moment you are in a strong position, Boadicea. But . . ."

Her voice was sharp now. "Do not use my name," she said, "until you have the right to do so. Only my chieftains have that right."

The tribune held back the words he had meant to say. Instead, he asked as simply as he could, "Do you expect me to become one of your chieftains, lady?" He tried to make it sound as bad as he could.

Her answer came back in a very low voice. She said, "Yes, Marcus. Of course you will do as I say. You will forget Rome, because Rome no longer matters, Rome is no longer alive in this province. But you will forget Rome for a better reason than that—because if you do not join me now I shall soon have you taken back to the glade where you will see Aranrhod go to the goddess Diana. We shall place you beside the stakes so that you will miss nothing, I can promise you that, tribune. And what you see will stay with you all your life, because you will know, as you hear her screaming, that with one word you could have saved her from that suffering. I can tell you, friend, it is not a pleasant thing that happens, and few of us who have seen it—we of the noble folk—ever forget it."

For many breaths now Marcus listened to the water dripping down the walls of that cave. He thought of his own sister. At last he said, "I think that I have become a coward, like poor Poenius Postumus at Glevum. I cannot stand against you. I cannot let Aranrhod die; she has hardly begun to live."

The queen whispered through the darkness, "She will not die, Marcus, if you will allow her to live. I swear on my husband's bones, I will never lay a hand on her if you will come with me and promise to help lead my armies against Rome. Only give me your promise. I ask no more."

Marcus prayed silently to his father, asking advice, and it seemed to him that he saw the gentle sad face of Ostorius the Tribune, nodding quietly, as though in agreement. He said, "Very well, lady, I promise to march with you until I might change my mind. I trust that my centurion will march with me and that Cynwas the Briton will be with his sister, and free."

The deep voice laughed above him, patiently now, even with understanding. She said, "You shall have your wishes, Marcus. But do not grow to be proud. Do not think, ever in your life, that I do what I do because of your Roman logic. I save your life now, and the little girl's, only because of one thing—that once, long ago, when you crossed my path before, I gave you my brooch and said it would keep you safe. I have not gone against a promise in my life and now is the wrong time to begin; now that I am almost the queen of Britain."

Marcus said, "Is that all, a bronze brooch? Does great Rome depend on nothing but that, a piece of twisted metal that I have almost thrown away a score of times?"

She said, "Not that alone, tribune. Life is never as silly as that, even for a Roman. But ever since I first met you, a little boy sitting on a horse too big for him, I have wished to have a son such as you were then; a proud boy, who would not budge even for a warband with swords and spears. And I never had a son. Two daughters, but not a son. Now do you begin to understand?"

But before he had begun to understand, he felt the wafting of her heavy skirts beside his face and then he was alone in that dark cave.

93

16

The Dark Gods

THE MARCH to Camulodunum seemed endless. Marcus went alongside Tigidius through the summer dust, now dressed in the war-gear of a tribal chief. He had allowed them to paint his face and body, and wore a tall wolfskin helmet which made him look like a giant. He even carried a horsehair fly whisk in his right hand, which no Roman had done before him, not even old Claudius who had spent so much time in Africa writing his histories of the campaigns.

He did not know where he might find Cynwas and little Aranrhod. He thought they were somewhere in the rear of the great column. The Queen Boadicea was away to the front in her death-cart. There were so many folk on the move now that it was impossible to see her since they had turned off the Ermine Street onto the narrower road to the veteran's colony.

Once, when they were not too pressed by the tribesmen, Marcus turned to the centurion and said, "Very well, I am sorry, just as sorry as you are. But this had to be done. I had to give my word or we would all have been dead; not only the little one, over the stakes and into the fire. Rome does not matter as much as the agony of the little girl, does it?"

Tigidius said, without looking to left or right, "We are not here to talk of little girls, tribune. I am as much a man as anyone and hate it when the children are hurt, but we are in this dark and savage island on serious matters. We are here to bring light where there was none before, and if some folk suffer pain, it is so that all folk shall see the light."

Marcus felt his nostrils flaring out at this and said sharply, "If she were your daughter, man! If you saw that happening to your daughter . . ."

Then he could not bring himself to say any more. He marched on in silence, flicking the summer flies from his face and pretending to whistle a tune. It was a tune he had made up to fill the silence, and he was not a good musician!

At last Tigidius smiled and touched his arm. "You have convinced me, tribune," he said. "Now stop whistling. It is worse than this parching dust to me."

Marcus replied gently, "Look, friend, you do not have to come to Camulodunum because I chose to give the woman my word. You did not swear an oath to her. You could run away at any convenient spot along this road. You could be safe. I do not hold you to your army oath."

Tigidius put on a cold face again and said, "Where you go, I go. All army oaths apart, I promised your father. So give your tongue a rest, boy. Let us see how things turn out."

Marcus forgot that he was a tribune then. He only remembered that Tigidius had known his father even before he had. He remembered also Tigidius had taught him all he knew about being a soldier, about being a Roman. When you thought about it, the two were the same thing.

So they went on down the straight road, choking with gray dust, hearing nothing but the dreamlike sound of feet and the low buzzing of the tribes, as though the bees of all the world were swarming at last. It was not a good sound and Marcus did not wish to be in the middle of it; but he could not think of anything else he might have done, and so he went with the tribes, trying to forget all he had previously known.

But at the end of the day there were some things he could not forget, and would never forget.

Ahead, at a distance of half a mile, lay the veterans' colony of Camulodunum. Always, up in the gray garrison at Lindum, soldiers had said how much they wished their time was done, so that they could retire to the new city of white houses and fountains and easy living at Camulodunum. There, they said, the senate saw to it that every man who had served his time under the eagles would find rest and contentment. In Camulodunum there were theaters and temples and villas, shops and taverns and public baths. A retired soldier on pension would feel that his twenty-five years of marching up and down the world had been worth while, a good investment of youth and strength. In Camulodunum, that soldier would think he had strayed onto the Elysian Fields.

But what Marcus saw now was not the heaven that had been promised.

Thick columns of black and oily smoke rose toward the late afternoon sky and dark red tongues of flame lay at ground level; black birds rose crying above the fires, as though they mourned for what they saw beneath them. It was all so strange, because just then a swift shower of summer rain came down without warning and was followed straightway by a rainbow that seemed to frame the burning city under its colored arch. It did not seem right that the gods should let this lovely arch lie over such a ruined place.

And when they saw it, the tribesmen all about drew in their breath and let out a long and menacing humming sound, as though the gods had spoken for them and not for the Romans.

Marcus said shortly, "Mithras is not with the veterans today. Let us push to the front and see what is happening. Perhaps there is man's work for us to do."

What they saw below, halted them. The city lay beside a sluggish river with each of its criss-crossed streets and almost every one of its buildings in view. Some of these had been humble, with square vegetable gardens and grazing for a cow or a few sheep; some had been tall and noble, fronted with columns of white stone and surrounded by dark cypresses. Now the swarming myriads of tribesmen sat on the earth at every side, watching and waiting and laughing, as though they were seated in some theater while a comedy was played for their amusement. They blackened the earth with their numbers. The city stood out in the midst of them like a child's toy, made small by the multitude.

It was no longer the city that veterans dreamed about. It was more like a neglected midden heap. The thatch had been burned from the humble houses and their garden walls thrown down. Cows and sheep lay butchered by the doors. The many-columned senate house stood gaunt and blackened now. Its tiled roof had slipped from the charred rafters and its pillars were either broken off short, or leaning against each other, as though one of the savage dark gods had brushed them aside with his hand. The painted amphitheater was now a heap of rubble, its seats flung down, smoke pouring from the windows all round its sides. Only one building still stood secure. From the statue above its portico Marcus could see that this was the temple dedicated to Claudius, the old emperor. But even here small dark men swarmed over the roof with torches, or ran at the great bronze-studded doors with battering-rams.

Tigidius said in a dull voice, "See, the statue of Victory in the square has been toppled. All the fountains have been overturned. They have even burned the cypress trees."

Marcus felt his eyes fill with tears. He glanced away from the temple and saw a group of red-haired Demetae flinging children into the sluggish river, their hands and feet bound. And when he turned from this, he saw women in a little courtyard holding their hands up to the sky and screaming, as though this was the only way in which they could speak to the god who looked over them. As he watched, tall men in black wolfskins broke in with lances and began slowly and carefully to silence all prayers.

The centurion came to Marcus and put his arm about the tribune's shoulders. "We cannot help them, lad," he said. "If we went forward now, we should not get as far as that red river before they put a lance into us too. Have courage, Marcus; what cannot be cured must be endured."

Marcus shook the centurion's arm away and brushed the tears from his eyes. Now his jaw was clenched so hard that it seemed to him he would never open his mouth again. One side of his face twitched so viciously that he almost cried out with the pain of it.

He looked up into the sky and there, high above Camulodunum, he saw that the clouds of black smoke had seemed to gather in the form of an enormous man with horns starting from his head, and a great axe in his right hand.

He said to his friend, "The place is well and truly lost, Tigidius, when the dark god himself comes to direct the bloodletting. I would have thought he could have left it to his thousands of savages to slaughter a few women and children and weary old men."

Then Tigidius took him hard by the wrist and swung him round. "Look, Roman," he said. "If you have never before seen a man in your life, you will see one now; one who was indeed suckled by the She-wolf, our Mother."

Marcus looked to where the centurion pointed and saw something that he would never forget. Above the river, in one of the square gardens of a ruined house, a gray-haired veteran stood on a heap of straw and turf with a wooden shovel in his hands. He used it like an axe on all who came at him; and each time a dark-faced enemy fell back, this old man laughed gently and called out a number. They heard his voice clearly from where they stood. "Nine," he called. "Now, come on little ones, and let me make it ten. What! Have I marched all the way from Persia to be denied ten? Why, when I was in my prime, lads, under the main eagle of the second, I could manage ten before I went back to the tents for my morning porridge!"

Marcus said shortly, "I am going to him."

But the centurion dragged him back. "You fool," he said, "you would never cross that river. Be still, he has made up his mind what will happen. He would not even thank you to rob him of this last moment. I have felt this many times, under the eagles in Batavia and Gaul and Africa. It is nothing. It is what a centurion expects at the end. This man was a centurion. Look at the way he sets himself. Boy, only a centurion stands like that!"

Now the dark tribesmen lay back in wait by the garden wall. Some of them were grinning up at the old warrior, others were feeling their arms and legs in pain. The vast crowds about the city and in the trampled fields, sat silent; their eyes wide, their mouths open. Many of them were weeping without shame.

Then in this strange moment of silence, the voice of Boadicea herself sounded on the heavy air. Marcus could not see where she was, but he heard her words plainly enough. She said, "Old man, old man, it is a waste of bravery for such as you to die. We of the Iceni would stand ashamed in the eyes of the Mother if we put an end to you. I beg you, come forward and take my hands in homage, and you shall be among the first of my captains."

But the old man only glanced toward her and laughed. Then, in a thin calm voice he said for all to hear, "Who is prating about the Mother? Is there no Mithras to call on? He is the man's god, the soldier's friend. Is there some stray cat among you yowling down there by the river? Let her come up here and have her tail trimmed!"

Now the tribesmen seated about the city began to smile

and then to laugh, at first quietly and then openly, so that their laughter swept across the city like a gust of wind.

And Marcus suddenly heard a thin squeal of the queen's bone whistle, and a short arrow stood out in the middle of the old veteran's grey linen tunic. He heard the little thud it made, though he was so far away, and thought he heard the old man draw in his breath.

For a while the veteran stood tottering on the heap of turf, still with his hands clenched about his shovel, still trying to laugh. And then even he had to listen to the dark god's summoning. He swayed and let his shovel fall. Then one of his legs gave way and caused him to totter backward down the heap. A dark-skinned man started forward, his lance in his hand, but the chieftain beside him struck this man a hard blow that sent him back like a beaten dog.

And so those in the garden and those about the city watched this old Roman go onto his knees and then onto his face and then spread out his thin arms, as though he knew at the last that he could not fight all the world. And all of them saw that he was still laughing when his face plunged suddenly into the straw.

And when this was over, the tribes about the city sighed and beat with their hands upon their hard thighs in admiration. And the sound they sent up stirred the birds from the trees for a mile on every side.

And before these birds had settled again, Marcus suddenly cried out, "What he can do, we can, brother! Come, let us try these British jackals." He started to run, and so Tigidius followed him.

17

Along the River

THEIR FEET drummed on the trampled earth. At first
the tribesmen did not seem to see them, for so many were
moving here and there with violence. Then a tall chieftain
wearing a bunch of eagle's wing-feathers cried out, "Where
are you going, brothers?"

Tigidius called back over his shoulder, "To the temple.
We wish to be there when the gates fall."

The chieftain laughed and waved them on.

Once they came upon a score of Coritani sitting in a
ring and throwing dice. They were too busy with their
game to do more than glance up; and then the two
Romans had leaped over the bent heads and were away
again.

A boy wearing a lynx-skin robe looked up at them for a
moment, idly threw a piece of flint toward them, then
went on with his occupation of sharpening a long holly
shaft into a thrusting-spear.

Then they were down by the river, gasping and bewil-
dered. Tigidius said, "Stop, tribune, stop! The madness is
over. We could do nothing if we swam across. Those in
the temple are doomed, just as the old man was. Two
unarmed men like us could not save one of them. We
should have given our lives for nothing."

Marcus swung round on him suddenly and struck him
on the neck, but the centurion took his hands and held
them to his sides. "Be patient, lad," he said. "We shall

serve them better by staying alive. Now, for once, let me lead the way. Follow me and ask no questions."

He set off, loping along the course of the river, waving and laughing whenever they came up to a group of tribesmen. They laughed back and shook their spears.

Marcus came up with the centurion and said, "What are we doing? Where are we bound for, brother?"

The centurion said briefly without pausing in his stride, "We are going to Londinium now, Marcus. We are going to warn the folk there so that this shall not happen again."

Marcus nodded and slowly went on ahead of the older man, leaping thorn bushes and pushing through the gorse.

Once they passed a line of seven tall crosses of pine with bodies hanging from them. Tigidius said, "They are barbarians. They have no respect for women. We have wasted out time trying to make them into human creatures."

Marcus ran with his eyes turned away. He said, "I pray to Mithras that Suetonius will eat them up. I pray that the legions will leave this place a desert when they come from Wales. It is an island of carrion crows. It is sodden with innocent blood. It is a haunted place. It can never prosper."

Then they swung away from the river and went among the first trees of a straggling grove. Now there were fewer tribesmen about, and what there were lay underneath the boughs drinking from skins or dancing to the flute and drum. Many of them wore the blood-sodden togas of dead Romans.

It was here they first ran into danger. At the far end of an avenue of oaks, three men stood leaning on their long spears, arguing and stressing their points with movements of their long thin hands. They heard the Romans thudding up the turf and stopped talking to gaze at them.

Tigidius called out to them, "Make way! Make way! We carry a message for the queen."

But the men stood where they were and did not move.

Then Marcus said, "These are not Iceni. They are Bibroci. Look at the gold throat-rings they wear. Look at the white horses painted on their shields."

The biggest of the men called out, "What queen? We have no queen. And you are not Iceni. You are the Romans. Stand."

Tigidius gasped as he ran, "Keep on, brother. One of us might get through."

And so they plunged at the men who blocked their way. Marcus did not see what happened, for now the sweat ran down into his eyes, blinding him. He was aware that the men had set themselves for the spear-cast, leaning back and swinging up their lances. He began to run zigzag like a hare, and knew that Tigidius was doing the same. He heard a spear drone past his head and bent low, scarcely avoiding the tree-boles at his left. Then he felt a great blow on his chest and almost fell with the wind knocked out of him. To his right he heard Tigidius crying out, "Stand away, you fools! We are going to your chieftain."

A man with long, black hair put out hands to hold him. For a moment Marcus saw clearly how carefully the hair was oiled and plaited. He even saw the design on the twisted gold about the man's neck. Then he struck out with a sideways movement and felt the hard edge of his left hand hit against that neck-ring, and heard the man cry out with pain. At his right he heard another cry, and then the centurion saying, "Run, run, Marcus! We are through them. We are away!"

Now his heart was thumping so hard that the Roman thought he would have to stop and fall onto the grass, whatever happened to him. But he kept on, and on, and on—until the trees grew thinner, and ahead of him he saw the dusty gray road that led southward toward Londinium.

Behind there was no sound of pursuit. In front, the land seemed empty and deserted.

Then he stopped and felt for the wound in his chest. But Tigidius laughed and said, "Truly, Mithras put his hand over you when that spear came, brother. I saw it turn about in the air and strike you butt-first. All you will have is a bruise. You should give thanks."

Marcus turned to him and smiled now. "It hurts more than the point would have done," he said. "Am I to give thanks for that?"

They leaned on a stone and laughed together, their dusty painted faces running with sweat, their chests heaving and their limbs trembling.

Behind them, a long way beyond the wood, the black smoke still rose high into the sky; but now it was thinnner, as though the upper breezes had carried much of it away, or as though there was little left to burn in Camulodunum.

Marcus said, "We must be on our way. These savages will not wait long, when they have put an end to the colony. It is the best part of sixty miles to Londinium, but with the aid of the god we shall get there in time to warn them. These barbarians cannot move on the march as fast as we can run."

The centurion nodded. "They are not real soldiers," he said. "They will halt here and there to burn the standing corn and to destroy the villages off the main road. With the god's help we shall be of some use."

So they set off again, running a hundred paces, then walking a hundred, so as to conserve their strength. Once they even sat down by a little clear stream and drank the water and plucked red berries from a bush. It was the first food they had had all day, and poor enough it was. But they gave thanks for it and then pressed on.

And toward evening they came to a part of the road that suddenly narrowed like a chariot track, as though it were not often used for heavy wagons. It fell down into a hollow and twisted so they could not see what lay ahead of them.

To their left the moorland of coarse, yellowish grasses fell away, with dark groves standing here and there on it, as far as the horizon. To their right, at the edge of the track, rose a steep bank of earth, overgrown with willow-herb and dock. At its top, stretching above the road, thorn and alder grew rank and charred stakes of straight pine stood leaning haphazardly toward the sky.

The sky itself seemed low and menacing. It was the time of sunset and a thousand floating clouds were tinged with deep red over their heads.

Tigidius shuddered and said, "This is a strange place; not the sort of place to lead a squadron into unless the scouts had combed it well before."

Marcus pointed to a rough hut that lay farther up the slope, its hide-roofing now blowing out in the evening winds. "I think it is some kind of shrine," he said. "One of their druid places, perhaps. They are set in such lonely places as this."

The centurion sniffed. "I smell something cooking," he said. "My mouth waters at such a smell. I think it is a wild pig. I have never cared for this British cooking or the flesh they eat, but at this moment I would not say no to anything. I will run up the bank and see what it is."

Marcus loped on. "You will not like what you find," he called back. "It will be an offering of some sort, on an altar fire. Do not bring any of it for me, whatever it is. And do not waste our time over it."

The centurion laughed and answered, "You can run on, boy. I will catch up with you, and when you see what I carry in my hand, you will wish that you had some of it too."

So Marcus set himself against the steep pitch of the road and panted on. He had gone the better part of half a mile before he realised that Tigidius was not coming on behind him. He stopped and looked back down the empty road into the darkening hollow. At first he was about to call out to the centurion; then he checked himself in case other ears heard him beyond the overgrown ramparts.

To himself in a low voice he said, "You fool, Tigidius. To put Londinium in danger for the sake of burnt pig. I shall have a word to say to you, centurion, when I reach you."

He turned about and ran down the slope again and did not stop until he came to the wooden shrine once more. Then he scrambled up the slope and pushed his way through the tangled weeds and brambles. The place was half-rotten with damp, the lintels of its low entrance green with lichen and overgrown with ferns.

"Tigidius, you stupid old man," he called. "Come out of there and let us be off."

But the centurion did not answer; so Marcus went forward, bending low to get under the door.

Inside, the place was dark and heavy with the smell of burned flesh. Marcus could make out the wood fire that glowed on a flat limestone ledge by the far wall. He moved toward it, groping, and almost fell over the body of Tigidius, who lay sprawled before the stone, face downward, his arms stretched wide, as though he were flying.

Marcus fell to his knees beside him and began to roll him over. Then his right hand came away sticky with blood and he drew back for a moment. His eyes grew used to the dimness then and he saw the deep axe-cut at the base of the Roman's skull. It had almost severed his head from his body.

For a long time Marcus sat staring, unable to believe that the centurion was dead. He kept saying to himself, "No! Oh no! He has faced too many arrows, too many spears. He cannot die like this. It is impossible for him to die like this, in a stinking hut by the roadside."

But at last Marcus knew that the centurion was dead and that no prayers would bring him back to life now.

It was dusk when he came out of the shrine. He could

see no one near the place. Once he caught a glimpse of eyes shining brightly from beyond the hedge of briars, but when he went toward them they vanished and he heard an old sheep lumbering away into the tall grasses that led to a dark forest.

So he went wearily down the slope again, hardly caring who waited for him at the bottom, and then turned his face once more toward Londinium and began to walk slowly along the lonely road.

It scarcely seemed to matter now what happened.

18

Under the Striped Awnings

IT was midday and the sun above the river Tamesa beat down as though it shone in Africa and not in Britain. Three men sat under blue-striped awning, fanning themselves and talking with many movements of the shoulders and hands. They were not Romans or Britons.

Behind them stood their stalls, waiting for whoever should come down the long straight dusty road that led from Londinium up into the empty distant places of the province. Behind the stalls lay many jumbled streets and wooden houses. Some of these had vine leaves before the doors signifying they were taverns for weary travelers; some, with hoists and pulley-blocks over the upper storys, told that they were warehouses for whatever merchandise floated into the wharfs of the river. And before the river stood the tall army supply-base—the square stone-built repository of grain, dried meat and hides—that would feed, and keep the legions marching on stout footwear. This was the only place that was protected by a palisade. It was not a stone wall, but constructed of wood, as though whoever set up this storehouse had not thought of war, but only of a peace that would last forever.

Beyond the warehouse lay the river, slow-moving, gray and littered with a thousand small craft passing up and down, or from the north to south bank; though there was little on the south bank to visit, but thatched settlements from which the wood-smoke rose lazily in the late summer air.

One of the men under the striped awnings drank from a red clay winejar and smacked his lips. He was a very big man, red in the face and with hair so fair that it looked almost white. He also had hair on his face, and a thick blue robe of wool with a white collar of fox fur which came from the far north. His eyes were blue, too, but much lighter than his robe; so light that they seemed to have little life in them. His hands and wrists were red and very clumsy and big. He did not seem the sort of man who would touch things lightly, or play the lyre. His voice as he spoke the Roman city-tongue, was as clumsy and big. He said, "Along the Baltic we trade with the club and the axe, my friends. We do not haggle as you Libyans do. My brother, Swart, and I went out last season and fleeced the villages up toward the Finnish marshes. The folk up there are savages. They root about under the trees for grubs. But they have good furs to trade. Amber is what they like for necklaces, so we took them amber and shook our axes at them. We came back with four wagonloads of good furs in return for three sacks of amber and one of jet. Next year, Nerthus willing, we shall go again—and then retire to a snug farmstead in Gotland."

There was a thin-faced, dry-voiced man beside him,

dressed in a dark robe, his deep-brown hair cropped close to the scalp. His eyes were a light gray and he spoke slowly and gravely. He said, "Please do not call me a Libyan. I have nothing against those people, but I must insist that you give me my proper designation. My name is Orosius and I am from Spain. My home is in a very pretty town called Gades, and my forefathers came there from Phoenicia—if you have ever heard of it. I have nothing against Libyans, who may be very fine fellows for all I know, but it is correct to give a man his proper heritage."

The third man nodded in agreement. He was very small and wore a white wrapping round his head and a white robe with a broad scarlet sash about his body. His face was the color of walnut stain and his eyes were as black as the jet about which the Baltic man had spoken. He said very gently, "In Armenia we do not speak of the Libyans. They may be men, for all I know, but we have a legend that they are all descended from apes, and so we do not speak of them."

The big northerner laughed and drank from the skin again. "And what do you say of us from the Baltic?" he asked heavily.

The Armenian shrugged his thin shoulders. "We do not speak of you either," he said. "We have a legend that all creatures north of the Caucasus are either bears, or wolves, or foxes. We cannot go beyond that."

The Spaniard half-turned his head and smiled down into the dust at a cricket which was sending out a great noise. He said, as if to himself, "Gades, Gades—there one sees true men. There one hears true speech. Here it is all the chatter of idiots."

The northerner suddenly said, "My name is Ochter and I have yet to meet the man I could not lay down with my axe." He looked around, as though he were challenging someone.

But the other two merchants smiled at one another and

did not answer him. Then the Armenian said quietly, "My own family take ancient names. My own is Ula Buriash, after some king of Babylon, I understand. But most men find that too much to say, and simply call me Ula. You may call me Ula if you so wish. It matters little to me what men call me, as long as I can sell my silver plates and tin images."

Orosius said in an off-hand manner, "We Spaniards bring heavier cargo. I'd back my olives and wine and my finely-stitched leather ware against any in the world."

For a moment Ochter, the Balt, glared at him, then said, "Where I come from we brew good ale, not this thin sour wine. As for your leather stuff, we take the natural furs and latch them together with good deerhide thongs. That is stitchery good enough for any true man."

He began to feel under his stool for the iron axe that lay there. Ula, the Armenian, smiled and nodded at him. "Of course, of course," he said quickly. "We both understand, don't we, Orosius?"

But the Spaniard was looking away again, as though he had lost all interest in the conversation.

The heavy silence stayed, while the Balt fumbled about in the dust and the Armenian quivered. Then another man came stumping up from the streets toward them. He was short and very fat. His iron pot-helmet hardly fitted his round shaven head and his leather armor was stained with sweat and creaked at every move he made, his bulging legs were covered with dirty linen breeches, strapped round with twisted hide that had once been dyed red, but now had little color at all about it.

In his hand he carried a very rough-shafted lance with a loose iron head that seemed about to fall off with every shake he gave it. He said, "Hey, you three, get inside the palisade."

The Spaniard looked up at him lazily and said, "We do not pack up our stalls until sunset. That is the law here. Are you asking us to break the law?"

The Balt had found his rough axe now and was holding it over his knees, jogging it up and down as though he did not know what to do with it. The Armenian was already on a stool, trying to reach the hooks of the striped awnings and cursing that he had given his slave the afternoon off from work.

Then the man in the pot helmet put his face close to that of Orosius and said, "So, you want to make trouble? You think that merchants have a law to themselves, do you? Well, look at this, fellow."

He held his poor spear up to the Spaniard's nose, shaking it. Orosus looked away, then said to the ground before him, "In my country a man would be ashamed to look at such a thing. Our boys have better prodders to go out pigsticking. What is your name, soldier? I would like to have a word with your commander later on."

The man in the pot helmet glared at him awhile, the sweat running down his upper lip, his face quivering under the iron cheek-pieces. Then he controlled himself and said, "I am Geir, decurion of the city militia. Does that satisfy you, outlander?"

Orosius spat into the gray dust. "If you are Geir," he said, pronouncing the name in disgust, "then you are not a Roman. You are most likely a northman of some sort. But not a Roman. Now, if you came to us wearing correct war-gear and speaking a name like Gaius, or Lucius, or even Tiberius, then we would have listened to you and have uprooted our stalls—although, as even you must know—our license, paid to the city treasurer, allows us to stay out here until the last rays of the sun make it difficult to see.

Then the big Balt spoke. With his axe in his hand he said thickly, "I had a dog once called Geir, and a mangy flea-bitten hound he always was. He never even caught as much as a hare. Show him a rat and he could run for his miserable life. Did you say your name was Geir, my friend?"

The militia-decurion stepped back and went very red in the face. He did not answer the Balt, but went over instead to Ula, the Armenian. "Now then," he said, "what have you to say for yourself? Didn't I tell you to get inside the city stockade? Well, didn't I? Answer me."

The slightly-built trader got down from his stool very slowly. Then he arranged his long sleeves and at last he looked up at the militiaman and said, "Geir, my friend, I am only a small man, but I have many kinsmen. They have houses in Byzantium, Smyrna, Alexandria and Rome. I have wives in Syracuse, Lutetia and even among the Frisians—and they all have brothers with long swords. Not one of my kinsmen would like it to be known that I, Ula Buriash, who bears the name of a king, was glared at by someone called Geir, who sweats in untanned leather and wears a helmet two sizes too small for his fat pig's head. They would come in their ships, bringing their long swords, as soon as they knew."

The decurion of militia began to say something, then stopped. He turned away from the small Armenian and said to the Balt, "We see eye to eye, brother. We are from the north. Would you kindly tell your friends that I am only doing my duty? I have news that a great army of Britons is coming this way to burn down the city. It is for your own good that my captain asks you to come inside the stockade."

The Balt flung his heavy axe into the air and caught it. He said, "Who are you to know what is our own good? I had a dog once called Geir, and he did not know what was for his own good. He went after an old wolf that started up from a thicket and got his ears chewed off at one bite. Was that for his own good? That was a very stupid dog, that Geir. Put a pot-helmet on his head and he would have looked exactly like you."

The militiaman turned away then, whistling and trying not to let the head of his spear rattle. Then suddenly his eyes brightened because down the long, dusty road came a man bent with weariness and weakness. He wore a jacket of roughly-stitched skin and no shoes on his caked feet. He staggered from side to side as he came, hardly able to keep his balance.

And as he came he waved his arms from side to side weakly and croaked, "Get inside. Get inside. They are coming. The Iceni are coming."

He fell face downward in the shadow of the striped awnings, still muttering. The decurion of militia poked at his blistered back with the spearpoint for a while and then began to kick him in the side to rouse him. But Orosius, the Spaniard, stepped forward and pushed the man Geir aside without any fear. "Stand away," he said. "This man is from my own country unless I have lost my ear for language."

He held out his hand for the wineskin and the Balt gave it to him without question. Then he rolled Marcus over onto his back and poured some of the liquid down his throat.

The militia-decurion said in fury, "Why, this is one of them! Look at the war paint on his face. Look at the scars on his body. He is a Briton. Have you lost your senses?"

Orosius glanced up at him once, with very cold and steady eyes. He said in a quiet voice, "Go back to your icebergs, you dolt. Go back to the howling dogs of the north, but do not presume to tell me that I cannot recognise another Spaniard."

For a time, the merchants looked down on the young man, as Orosius cared for him. Then they packed up their stalls and moved down through the houses toward the slow river.

And when life seemed to come back into the young man's cheeks, Orosius stood away and said to the decurion, "Now he is your responsibility. See that he is cared for, or I shall come looking for you, and I have almost as many kinsmen as our friend Ula. Almost, though not quite. I have only one wife; but she has three brothers, and not one of them is smaller than I am."

He rose and called on porters to dismantle his stall. Then he went gravely down into the city.

Geir stood above Marcus for a while, then poked him with the end of his spear and said, "Come on now, my lad. Onto your feet, now. If you are what they say you are, we can put some war-gear on you and use you. We might even find a club for you to use, if the supplies have not run out. That is, if you have any idea of what real fighting is, though, from the rough look of you, I doubt it. Come on, then. Up with you."

He prodded again and Marcus rose and followed him, too exhausted to protest any longer.

19

Militiaman

L IFE was not easy in the supply base station. Marcus was given a roughly shaped club of bog oak, a pair of sandals too large for him, and a leather cuirass that stank of its last three owners and was covered with dried blood. To guard his head he wore a turban of wool wrapped about a rusty iron ring.

When he protested to Geir, his decurion, that man turned and called out to the slaves who were on their knees scrubbing the garrison floor, "See who has come among us! A great warlord, too proud to wear garments in which our other lads have died."

114

The slaves pointed their gnarled fingers at Marcus and laughed. When Geir made a joke in that place, they knew it was best to laugh, whether they understood his thick speech or not; and most of them did not, since they came from Gaul and the forested areas of Germany.

One of them, a raw-boned youth from the distant northern islands, with lank, ashen hair and stony eyes, even got up with his scrubbing brush in his hand and advanced on Marcus, shouting, "Come, warlord, I challenge you to combat—you with your fine weapon and I with my scrubbing brush. Let us see whose gods are the stronger."

But then Geir became angry and beat the Frisian youth aside with his belt buckle. Walking up to Marcus he said, "You see where your pride will get you? It will make you the laughing-stock of slaves. Now be obedient and try to learn the discipline of a true soldier."

Marcus felt his own anger rising and was about to say that he had once been an officer, a tribune of the ninth; but he knew that Geir would not believe him. So instead he said calmly, "I have carried arms before. I have worn armor. I have stood where the arrows whined. But I would not ask any man to stand under the arrows with such gear as you have given me."

The vein in Geir's red neck began to throb. As soon as he could get his voice again he said, "You, you starved bean-pole! What armor could you wear? What weapon could such as you carry? What arrows have you ever seen, but the sticks that young boys shoot in play?"

Marcus held his breath then answered, "Look, I am not here to be mocked. I came a long way down the dusty road to be of service to Rome. I did not come to have kitchen slaves point their fingers at me. Take me to the captain of this garrison. I will put my case to him in the Roman way."

Geir started to say something else to the listening

slaves. Then he thought better of it and swung on Marcus with a wicked smile.

"Very well," he said. "You shall go to the captain, and by sunset I shall hope to be present when he has the hide flogged off your mutinous back, you scum of the roads."

They went along many passageways until they came to a rudely-planed oak door, Marcus stayed outside under guard and the decurion went inside to make his complaint. While the decurion was away, one of the militia who stood beside Marcus leaning on a crooked lance said, "You've picked the wrong day for trouble, recruit. Old Marius the Belgian is in command. He'll tickle you up with the whip. Make no mistake about it."

He winked at his companion and made a great pretense of leaning against the wall with laughter. Marcus watched him for a time, then said, "What's wrong with your legs, man? Can't you stand up straight without the help of a wall?"

The two guards were helpless with mockery when Geir came back and pushed Marcus roughly inside the low room. "Good luck to you, you spying hound," he said. "May the gods have mercy on your worthless hide."

Marcus saw a little hunched man sitting at a dirty table with many stained papers before him pretending to read, and making crude marks with a reed pen in the margins. For the space of ten breaths he did not look up. Marcus had time to note his bald head, his badly bitten fingernails, his patched tunic and the poor quality of the weapons which leaned against his chair.

At last he said, "I have a report to make, captain."

The man scratched on aimlessly, then at last blew out his breath noisily and said, "Did you speak, recruit? Can such as you actually speak?"

Marcus repeated gently, "I have a report to make, captain. I think that you should hear it."

The man began to pick his teeth with the point of the reed pen. His eyes were red-rimmed and filmy. A trickle of moisture ran down onto his cheek, but he did not seem to mind it.

He said at last, "You are offal from the streets. Your father was offal before you. If the truth were told, judging from the marks upon your body, you are a runaway slave. What report has a runaway slave to make to anyone, much less to a captain of militia?"

Marcus felt the pulse beating in his forehead, but he clenched his hands and did not raise his voice.

"Captain," he said, "I am not what I seem. I have been more than I seem, and I have important news to give to one in authority. I ask you to listen to me, for the fate of the city may depend on it."

Marius the Belgian got up from his chair and went to the window. There he stood, picking his teeth and gazing out. At last he turned, his lips drawn in, and said, "I am an old soldier. I have seen much service in Rome's cause. I can judge a man when I see one. What do you say to that, you upstart byre-cleaner?"

Marcus grasped his hands in front of him tightly, so that he should not run at the man and strike him down. He said in a low voice, "I am not here to exchange insults with you. But I can tell you that Marius the Belgian does not figure on any army-list of the three legions with which I am familiar. It is a name unknown to me. But that is of no importance. It matters only that you should be aware of the danger that threatens, and should take precautions."

Marius did not give him time to finish what he had to say, but almost leaped at him and struck him across the cheek with an iron spatula that lay on the table. Then, as Marcus staggered back, the captain yelled out, "Take him away! Take him away! He has threatened me with violence."

Geir and the two guards ran in, flailing their spear-shafts. Marcus went down, unable to defend himself, and lay still while they beat and kicked at him.

At last they flung a bucket of water over him, then dragged him down to a cellar underneath the guardroom and rolled him onto a pile of damp straw. The place was dug out of the earth and smelled of decay. There was no window-hole to let in air, so he did not know how long he lay there, hungry and thirsty, and feeling the pain of his wounds more sharply than ever.

In the darkness he saw Tigidius; Aranrhod awaiting sacrifice in the wood; Boadicea blowing her bone whistle for the old soldier to be shot at Camulodunum. He even saw his father, in the distant days when he was a tribune at Lindum. Now his father seemed very sad, as though everything had turned out wrong with Rome.

Marcus had a fever from his wounds, and shuddered till all his body shook, down there in the damp earth. It was like being buried alive, and the fever brought him nightmares in which he screamed and yelled until someone beat on the trapdoor and told him to be a man and take his suffering bravely.

Then one morning they let him out again, and even helped him to climb up the rickety wooden ladder to the guardroom. And there, Geir was waiting with a staff in his hand. He said, "Perhaps you have learned your lesson now, byre-slave. If you have, then put on your gear again and we will see if we can make a soldier of you after all. At a time like this, we need all the men we can get, even poor scarecrows like you."

So Marcus put on his poor war-gear and marched about the city with the other militiamen, who had no more spirit than beaten dogs. Not once did he see a true Roman, a man of the legions, not even when he was set to mount guard over the big grain-warehouse from which the army drew all its supplies.

Only one of the other militia would deign to speak to him. He was a youth named Gnithus, who had a shriveled right arm that flapped about helplessly as he walked.

He was an orphan and had no kinsmen in Londinium, but claimed to have many friends in important positions. One night, as they lay down in their blankets outside the supply-base, Marcus said to him "Look, Gnithus, if you have such friends, will you please get to one of them on your day off and warn him that the Icenian queen has raised all the eastern tribes and is on her way to burn this city to the ground? Will you, for the love of Rome?"

Gnithus gazed at him blankly for a moment. Then he said, "Rome does not need such spies as you to save her. Rome is great and will last forever. The Icenian queen and all her tribesmen and their like will fade before us when we march against them. Now go to sleep."

But Marcus took him by his sound arm and shook him. "Look, friend," he said, "I can tell from your speech that you have always lived in this place. I can tell that you are not a soldier. I beg you, listen to me and take word to someone in authority that the tribes are massing like birds before they fly away at the year's end. They are coming in countless swarms. They have burned Camulodunum to ashes. They have almost destroyed the ninth legion. In this poor town, can such as us stand against those who have made Petillius Cerialis turn tail and gallop off?"

Gnithus sat up, his blanket about him, and said, "They all say that you are a liar and a rogue. I was the only one who would talk to you, because being lame and mocked at I needed a comrade. But now, even I can see that you are a mischief-maker. I can see why none of the others will speak to you, and why our decurion spits when you pass near to him."

Marcus tried to smile. "Gnithus, my comrade," he said, "forget all that. Just rise now and go to one of your important friends—it does not matter which—and tell him that you have spoken to one who has seen Boadicea's army on the march. Fetch him to me and I will tell him the rest. Then, with the help of Mithras, he will go to the magistrates and we shall get something done here before they come upon us."

Gnithus drew back his lips and laughed mockingly in the face of Marcus. "You traitor," he said. "You have seen the tribesmen because you are one of them. I will get up from my bed, to be sure, but it will not be to warn one of my important friends in the city. They are men of trade and need their sleep. I will tell someone, though, I can assure you of that."

He rose and shambled away. Soon afterward four militiamen came back with him and dragged Marcus to his feet. He was too weak now to wrestle with them, and let them drag him before Geir once more.

The decurion was sitting in a tent beside the broad river, beating on the table with a riding whip. When the men flung Marcus before him he hardly looked up, but said, "He is a madman. Only a madman would prate on so about Boadicea and her armies. The poor fool's wits have been turned by something or other. I am a merciful man. There is no use in beating him further. That will not put sense into his thick head. Take him out by the city gates and tie him up to a stake. There his hot brain will be cooled, and he will be the first to see this Boadicea of his, if she does come. That should satisfy the fool."

Then he turned round and called out to a slave to fetch in the Saxon girl, Gerd, to sing for him and pass the time away.

And when they dragged him out, Marcus felt that truly he must be what they said he was, a slave and a coward, for now he had no more heart left in him to fight, and no more pride.

20

Gerd and the Merchants

THE DAY was hot again and the flies buzzed about Marcus in a black swarm. He could do nothing to send them away. His bound wrists were lashed above his head. His feet scarcely touched the ground. The stake they had tied him to was of rough pine that tormented his bare back with its bark and knots. But this was not as bad as the flies. They walked across his wet face and explored his nostrils. He had not strength enough to snort them away now. The arrow wound in his shoulder felt as hot as fire, and there was a deep ache in his chest from the spear blow.

A rough-coated dog came sniffing toward him, then saw that he was alive and stopped, snarling, his hair bristling. Marcus said in a whisper, "Wait a little while longer, comrade. I shall not go away, I promise you."

Four boys came with stones and drove the dog away. Then they sat under the tall pine stake and gazed up at Marcus, not cruelly, but with curiosity. They spoke a very fair Latin, but from his half-shut eyes, Marcus saw that they were British of one sort or another—probably from among the woodland Cantii, he thought, judging by the iron-work of their belt buckles.

The oldest of them, a red-haired boy with freckles under his blue eyes, said, "I will bet that he will die before tomorrow. I will lay my iron dagger on it."

The other boys laughed. One of them said, "Tomor-

121

row! Why, this one is strong enough to last till Suetonius gets here—and that could be the day after. They are very strong, these Romans. My father says that you can stick a spear through them, and they *will* not die. He knows, he has done it many times."

The red-haired boy scoffed. "Your father," he said, "has never even seen a Roman, that old man. He has never put a spear to anything bigger than a wild dog. He has never even faced a wolf, much less a Roman."

They lost interest in Marcus then and began to play at dice in the dust. Marcus tried to call out to them, to ask them for a cup of water, but his throat was too dry and at last he gave up trying.

Then the red-haired boy got up from the ground and strolled over to him, whistling and not looking into his face. He said to the others, "Hey, he has a little pouch behind his belt. There might be something in it. If we took what was in it, no one would know, and he will not want it any longer."

Marcus made a great effort as the boy's fingers searched in the pouch and he groaned out, "Behave yourself, fellow. You speak like a Roman, behave like one. Get away from me."

The boy stared up at him in astonishment. Then he turned to the others and said, "He is still alive. He can talk. Listen to him. He can still say words."

But Marcus had not the force left in him to speak again. He shut his eyes and heard the boys moving around him, slapping the pine stake and even trying to rock it in the ground. One of them said, "He is a Greek slave from Verulam. You can tell by his face and the marks on his body. He has had a harsh master and has run away to find work on a ship here. They often do. You can tell that. He must be a thief for them to hang him up like this. Greeks are great thieves, and they always tell people to behave."

122

The red-haired boy said, "Greeks are the biggest liars in the world. Not even Romans can tell as many lies as Greeks can, though they try hard enough."

Marcus was wishing that at least the boys would whisk the flies away from him, but they did not. Then he felt their hands dragging at his belt, and one of them feeling into the small deerskin pouch at his back. He tried to draw his body away from their fingers, but only swung on the hide-thongs. He heard them laugh at this, then one of them cry out, "Look what was in the pouch. It is a brooch. See, it is a bronze brooch, shaped like a stag leaping. This is worth something. The Greek must have stolen it. Now it is mine."

Suddenly he saw himself as a little boy, sitting on a horse in the sunken lane and the fierce queen handing this brooch to him. He had lost everything but this brooch, and now these boys were taking it away from him. In a strange way, he felt that once the brooch had been taken, he would have lost everything in his life. He would be ready to die. With a great effort he opened his eyes and growled, "That is mine. A queen gave it to me. It is mine."

The three boys turned toward him and began to laugh, pointing at him. "A queen! A queen!" the red-haired one mocked. "What queen, slave? Why should a queen give her brooch to a slave?"

And all at once Marcus felt the salt tears running down his cheeks. This was the final fall, he thought. This was what a man could come to, a soldier even, a tribune of the ninth. And now he wished that he could be dead, so that he could forget all the things that troubled him, all the pride and strength he had lost, all the friends he had lost.

One of the boys said, "See, the Greek is weeping! He is a grown man, but he is weeping. We British do not weep like these cowardly outlanders."

Then suddenly from behind him, Marcus heard swift footsteps running, and a sharp voice calling out, "Leave the man alone, you little rogues. What have you taken from him, you alley robbers! Give it back!"

A girl of perhaps sixteen came rushing at them, her light golden hair flying, a stick in her hand. She had her blue gown tucked up above her knees and could move faster than any of the boys.

The red-haired one cried out, "It is the Saxon, look out, comrades."

Another one said, "Do not hit us, Gerd, we were only looking at the brooch. We did not mean to steal it. He said we could look at it."

But she did not listen to them. Her stick flailed about and landed many times on backs and legs and shoulders. They flung down the brooch and ran away, threatening that they would bring their brothers or fathers, and that she would be sorry for what she had done before the day was out. But she called certain things after them that made even Marcus start with shock.

Then she turned to him, the brooch in her hand, and said in quite a different voice, "Shall I put the brooch inside your tunic—what is left of it? It might be safer there."

He looked down on her and tried to smile. She reminded him more of his sister, Livia, than anyone he had seen. Then, in another light, she was like Aranrhod, only older. Her eyes were deep blue and set wide apart. Her nose was straight and thin. Her mouth was quite broad and turned up at the corners as though she would rather laugh than cry. Marcus thought that she was very pretty. Wryly, he thought that if only she were scrubbed and put into fine clothes instead of this ragged-hemmed gown of dirty blue wool, she might even be beautiful. With rings on her fingers and a gold collar about her neck, she could pass for the daughter of a Senator.

He said to her, "I have no further use for the brooch, girl. Take it as a gift from me, for driving the boys away."

The girl looked at the bronze stag in her narrow palm, then back at him with puzzled wide eyes. She said hoarsely, "You do not mean it. No one would give away such a brooch. I cannot take such a fine thing. What would I do with it? Someone would kill me for it. I own only what I stand up in, and this distaff. They would know and would kill me, the night-robbers."

Marcus said, "Very well, put it into my tunic. But I would like you to have it when they take my body down from this stake."

She wafted the flies from him, then began to scratch her head and bite her lip. Gazing up at him she said, "I am of the Saxones, and my village is by the river Albis. My name is Gerd, and I have warriors for my father and brothers. Not one of my kinsmen has died in his bed for ten generations. We trace our family back to Woden."

Marcus almost smiled then, but thought better of it. He nodded gravely and said, "That is a fine record, Gerd. Tell me, are you a slave here in Londinium?"

She shook her tangled head and said proudly, "We of the Saxones have never been slaves. If they tried to make slaves of us, we should cut out throats with a piece of flint, or should make ourselves starve to death rather than serve them. I came on a ship to this place when my village died in the drought last year. My cousin Brand brought me and set me on the shore. He is a good man and a pirate. His ship lies off the island of Vectis through the summer. He gets good pickings from the Roman ships that pass back and forth. They are very stupid, the Romans."

Marcus said, "I am a Roman, believe it or not."

Gerd stared at him and said without smiling, "I thought you were a British warrior from the way you speak. But now I think you must be a Roman, to be so stupid and hang up like this. You have many cuts and bruises on you, but they will not kill you. I have seen worse wounds on my father and my brothers and they always lived—until the drought came and killed them. Always they brought their wounds to the women of the village. My mother knew all the cures, and gathered herbs for various wounds. No, you will not die unless they starve you to death on this stake."

She tore a length from the hem of her robe and wiped the sweat from his face. Then she looked round to where the three merchants were having their stalls set up, just by the wooden gates of the city.

Suddenly she began to walk away. "Do not be afraid," she said, "I am not leaving you. I will come back."

After a while the three merchants left their stalls in charge of slaves and came walking toward the stake, led by Gerd who tried to hurry them along. Marcus even thought she would strike at them with her distaff.

Orosius came to him first, smiling, and said, "I wondered what had happened to you, Spaniard. I have looked for you in the streets. They seem to have taken a dislike to you. Well, at least I can fetch you a cup of wine and some honey-cakes that I had thought to eat myself at midday."

Ochter, the Balt, said gruffly, "This fellow would do better eating a piece of beef and drinking a horn of northern ale. That would put the heart back in him."

Gerd pushed him aside. "He is too weak to eat and drink like you fat folk," she said sharply. "Stand aside and let the Armenian put salve on his wounds."

Ochter smiled at her and said, "You speak like a true woman of the northland. If I had a daughter like you, I would be a proud man. Does your master want to sell you? How much does he want for you?"

But she was not listening to him. She was almost dragging Ula Buriash forward by the sleeve of his robe.

And after a while, when the Armenian had put oint-

126

ment into the shoulder wound and had bound Marcus about the chest with tight strips of linen, Ula Buriash said, "Such cures ask for payment. Has he anything to give in return?"

Gerd swung on him in fury. "What!" she said, her eyes and nostrils wide. "You dare to ask such a thing from one who cannot help himself? Are you a true man or another sort of thief?"

The Armenian held out his hands and raised his shoulders in protest. The other merchants smiled and nodded at her in agreement. Orosius said, "Ula is only teasing, girl. He is always the same. Bargaining is in his blood, but he means no harm."

Then Gerd turned on him and said, "And you, what will you do for this man? Will you buy him and set him free?"

Orosius said gravely, "I would, if he were for sale, little one. But I think that he is being punished for something, and if I interfered, I would lose my license to trade here. You understand, a merchant is at the mercy of the city authorities. He cannot always do as he would wish."

Gerd spat in the dust. "Licenses, mercy!" she said. "City authorities! They are just words, merchant. Show that you are a man, and buy him. Then you can set him free again."

The Spaniard's face was troubled. He said slowly, "I cannot break the law, little one. How can you ask me to break the law of the land I trade in?"

Gerd almost struck him with the stick, but suddenly the big Balt, Ochter, took her by the wrist and said, "There, war-maiden, you are too ready with that distaff of yours. Try to learn that you can get your own way without beating out the brains of all who hold another opinion."

Then he passed her by, and taking a sharp knife from his robe, bent and cut the thongs that held Marcus by the ankles. So, holding his arm about the Roman to support

127

him, he reached up and slashed away the wrist thongs, then let Marcus slide gently to the ground.

They all looked at Ochter in surprise, but he only smiled, wiped the blade of his knife and put it away again.

"I shall sail out of Londinium on the afternoon tide," he said thickly. "I do not think there is any more trade to be done now. There are other markets a man may trade in. Britain is not the only place in the world, thanks be to Woden. I think I shall pack up straightway, and if I can find a comfortable boat, set up my stall somewhere in Gaul."

He said no more but walked back slowly toward the striped awnings.

Orosius said then, "Well, we have broken the law, and we cannot mend what we have broken. If you two would care to take ship with me, we will sail down to Gades. I do not think anyone will molest us. The seas are very quiet, I hear, at the moment."

Gerd looked at Marcus, but he shook his head. "I must stay," he answered. "I would like to see Gades, but I must stay."

Then Gerd said, "I must stay too. This man needs someone to look after him. Besides, I have promised to meet my cousin Brand later in the year. He has a business off the island of Vectis."

Orosius smiled thinly. "I have heard of his business," he said. "It is something to do with shipping, I understand."

Gerd gave him a stern glance. "Yes, it is," she said. "And on your way down to Gades he might even do business with you, merchant."

The Spaniard shrugged his shoulders. "He will find that I drive a hard bargain," he said. "I do not travel without protection. Your cousin Brand might find himself sailing back to Germany without his shirt."

Then suddenly another thought seemed to strike him. He said gently to the girl, "Come with me to my stall. I

128

have a shirt and a few other things that would fit this man. If he is to stay in the city, he had better be dressed so that Geir and his watchdogs do not recognise him again."

And when Gerd had helped Marcus on with the gray shirt and green woolen cloak and hood, he looked a different man. But Ula Buriash shook his head and smiled. "No," he said. "It is good but not good enough. A sharp-eyed rogue like Geir would pick him out. Come, lead him to my stall. I will show you how it should be done."

There Marcus sat under the awning while Ula dyed his hair a chestnut color and then wiped walnut stain on his face and limbs. And when the Armenian had finished, Gerd stood back and laughed. "Why, he looks like an African," she said. "He has just come up from the deserts, I am sure. Tell me, African, where are your camels then?"

But Ula Buriash had no more time for jesting. Quickly, he made his servants pack up the stall and put it on a handcart. As the merchants went down toward the river, they waved at Marcus and Gerd.

"Come with us, if you wish," said Ochter. "There are better places to be in than this midden heap, you know. I could show you cities where even the slaves wear silver and silk. You would never believe it."

Once more Gerd looked up at Marcus, as though she wished to go with the merchants, but his face was as set as it ever had been. So she shook her head and waved farewell to the traders.

Then, taking Marcus by the hand, she led him from that place before the militia made their morning tour of duty. She knew every lane and alleyway in the city, and they met no one but market-porters and masons carrying their tool bags to the new sites on which they worked.

21

Governor-General

THEY SAT in the straw beside an open window in the deserted upper story of an old warehouse beside the river. Far down below them Marcus saw craft of all sizes pulling out along the Tamesa, some with sails that bellied in the evening breeze, others rowed by men who seemed anxious to be away. Gerd brought him a wooden platter of meat scraps and barley bread. At first he shook his head, but she grew so angry with him that he ate it all to the last crumb. And then he said, "It is a long time since anyone commanded me, Gerd. No doubt I shall get used to it in time."

She brushed the damp hair from her eyes with her dusty hand. "That bread and meat took some getting," she said smiling and showing her very white teeth. "I had to run half over Londinium on errands to get it. So I could not bear to see it wasted after all that."

Then she lay back in the straw and began to laugh. "You look so different," she said. "I cannot believe a man could look so different with his hair dyed and his face blacked! Among my folk the men black their faces when they go to war—but you do it so as to stay at peace. You are a funny man, Marcus!"

Then Marcus began to laugh too, although he had enough sorrow in his heart to weigh him down for a lifetime. He said, "You would not think I was a funny man if you saw me on my horse in my armor, with my tall

130

war-helmet on and my long sword at my hip. You would not laugh if you saw me coming at you, with the soldiers behind me glaring over their tall shields and their lances pointing at you."

But this made her laugh more than ever. The tears ran down her face and made little clean runnels. She said, "You, on a horse! Oh! Oh! Oh! And with armor, no! You are teasing me again. You are the funniest man. You are like my cousin Brand. He pretends that he has sailed down to Egypt and back again before breakfast. He talks about the great tombs there, and the camels—as though he has really seen them. He is a funny man too. But not as funny as you are. You are funnier than anyone else in all the world, I am certain."

Marcus laughed again. He had not felt as happy as this for years; probably not since his father used to take him out riding, or since he used to play with Livia and the Africans on the sea shore at Carthago Novo. Mithras, but it was good to laugh again and be happy. He had forgotten what it was like, to do this simple thing.

He said, "Tell me about Brand. Is he clever and handsome like me?"

Gerd was chewing at a piece of straw and did not look at him now. She said slowly, "You are not clever, or you would not have let those fools tie you up to the stake. And as for being handsome, you are more like a hawk than a man. Look at your fierce eyes and your beaky nose! Brand has pretty green eyes. I think they are green. They change as the sea changes when he stares down at it to see if there are rocks under the keel. And his nose is nice and solid. A man from the Frisian islands hit it with an oar once when they quarreled over a ship they had taken, and the oar made his nose very square and solid. A pleasant flat nose. I liked it so much, I promised to marry him and be his wife when he has made his fortune robbing the Romans off Vectis."

Marcus said, "I hope you are happy with Brand, Flat-nose. I hope you have ten sons, all with flat noses."

Gerd threw her straw away and said, "I would like daughters, all tall and beautiful, with good hands for the horses and for making pastry. I do not want sons, because when they went from the steading with their swords I should worry about them every minute till they got back. I have seen the men come back to my village, Marcus, and I have grown to be sick and weary of what I saw. They sing and boast and drag carts full of plunder—but they are always hurt—always coming back to be looked after and healed. And they are never the same again. These warriors are as silly as the boys who mocked you down by the stake. They kill themselves quickly, or slowly; but they kill themselves. I want daughters when I have a family of my own."

Marcus wanted to tell her that he was a warrior too; and that if he was only clever enough, a warrior did not have to come back hurt every time out. But then he thought of the men he had been with—and they were all dead now. Even Petillius Cerialis, a leader of great warriors, was shut up in Lindum, sweating in terror of the tribes. He thought of his father and of Tigidius. And Tigidius had gone away so quickly, without any glory, without anything—just reaching out for a piece of burned swine-flesh. . . So he said nothing.

And then, just as the sun was sinking fast, he heard a great shouting outside down in the square, and the howling of horns and the clattering of horses' hooves, and the thick murmuring of crowds. He went to the window-hole and said, "Something is happening."

Gerd nodded lazily. "It is the Governor-General coming in. He has ridden from the far side of Britain to be here, with just a few horse-soldiers. They were talking about it in the market while I was running errands to get your meat and bread. The folk down there say that he is a madman to risk so much, riding through the wild country to Londinium. They say there is nothing for him here."

Marcus said, "You mean that Suetonius Paulinus has come into the city? Suetonius?"

Gerd rose from the straw and screwed up her eyes. "I do not know what his name is," she said. "All Roman names sound the same to me. But I can tell you that he is the general who has come from killing priests in Mona. And now he thinks that he can rule Londinium with his army ways, but he cannot. That is what the folk in the streets say. They say that he may be a general, but he cannot tell people what they have to do and where they have to go. The folk here are not soldiers to be ordered about by some general they have never seen, and don't want to see, either."

Marcus said quietly, "But he is a great one. He is one of the greatest men living in this world, Gerd. If they only knew that, they would do as he says."

Gerd said, "How do you know that he is great? What do you know about such men?"

Marcus said, "I have always known the general. He was a friend of my father's. When I was a little boy, Suetonius took me on his white horse, in front of him, and we rode up and down the ranks of the twentieth legion. The men all cheered and waved their javelins. I shall never forget it. It was like riding in front of the god. And afterward Suetonius took me into the mess and with his own hands poured me a glass of wine and water; with his own hands, Gerd. How could I ever forget such a man?"

But she was nibbling at strands of her hair and was not listening. Then she said, "They are coming in now. There is an old gray-haired man on a badly-kept pony in front. Is that the great Suetonius? Is that the god?"

Marcus hobbled to the window and gazed down. It was Suetonius, but he seemed so much smaller now. His back was bent too, and his legs looked thinner as they dangled down. Even his gear was dull and neglected. And the men who rode behind him looked like scarecrows or forest brigands.

Gerd said, "I do not understand Romans. They make so much of so little." Then she turned away and went back to the straw.

But Marcus shouted out, "Up the legions! Paulinus! Paulinus!"

And for a short instant, the general seemed to hear his voice, and looked up from the street right into his eyes. But there was no understanding in those eyes, no friendship, no recognition. And the cavalcade passed on beneath the window, into the crowds of silent citizens who did not wish to be disturbed by generals or by anyone.

Marcus turned away from the window and saw that the girl was looking at him, smiling and smoothing her hair. She said, "I did not hear him greet you, Marcus. He should have greeted one who rode before him and took wine from his cup. Why was that, do you think?"

Marcus sank down beside her wearily. "It is this color on my face," he said. "He did not know me as this color."

He waited awhile and then suddenly he punched one hand into the other savagely and said, "I wish to Mithras that I did not skulk like a coward with this black face. I would rather go with my own face and die, as long as my general greeted me."

But Gerd shrugged her shoulders and turned away. Then she began to sing a low mournful song about a lost child in a deep German forest where the only light came from the glow of wolves' eyes.

22

The Doomed City

THAT EVENING as twilight came down over the doomed city, Marcus was still muttering in the straw, accusing himself of betraying the general, and saying that he should have gone down to meet him and tell him of the great danger that was coming. He refused to drink a bowl of milk that Gerd had got from a goat tethered in a nearby yard. He knocked the wooden bowl from her hands and told her she had kept him from his duty, by putting him up there in the deserted warehouse and causing him to live like a coward. The girl stood so much of this, then hardened her face and said, "Very well, Roman, if you think you are so much of a man, go to the general. Go now; you know the way down the stairs. But when he hangs you as a deserter, or the people stone you as an Icenian spy, do not look around for me. I shall not come to save you the second time."

Marcus got up from the straw and said stiffly, "When a tribune depends for his life on a Saxon, and a young girl at that, he has sunk low. He has ceased to be a man."

She smiled and nodded at him gently, and watched as he turned and went toward the hanging door of the place. There he had to put out his hand to steady himself, but he missed the lintel and fell forward almost into the dark well of the stairway.

Then she jumped up and ran to him and dragged him back, shaking her head and smiling sadly. "Oh, Marcus," she said, "oh, poor Marcus!" He frowned awhile, then gave up the struggle and let her help him to the straw. And, as she was doing this, they heard the sound of folk gathering down in the city square below, and then a great bull-like voice speaking through a leather trumpet, a Roman voice.

It said: "Citizens, men and women of Londinium, hear me, hear me!"

The crowd was silent, and then the voice went on. "Our Governor, Suetonius, bids me tell you this, and these are his words: The enemy are coming in great force to take this town. They will burn and kill and we cannot prevent them, for Londinium is a peaceful place and has no walls or fortifications, nor have we enough soldiers to hold the enemy back. We have the militia, it is true, but they are few and poorly armed. We have a squadron of cavalry, but they are spent with riding across Britain and could scarcely face the hordes that come upon us. It was the hope of our Governor that the second legion would be here to protect you but they are held at Glevum by their own enemies and cannot march out to our aid. The fourteenth and twentieth are on their way, but they cannot get here before the Iceni do. I tell you our case so that you shall know I hide nothing from you. Have courage, be brave, be Romans."

Just then voices called out, asking what use bravery was if they were to be slaughtered like bullocks in a butcher's yard. But the Roman herald ignored these cries and went on: "If a legion cannot hold a position, it moves to another one and draws the enemy with it. And this we shall do. It is the Governor's intention to withdraw from Londinium soon, and with the help of the gods meet the enemy at another place, and so destroy all who stand against Rome. Citizens of Londinium, have faith. The tribes may burn our city, but we shall build another when we have defeated them, and defeat them we shall. Hail, Nero! Hail, Suetonius!"

136

There was little cheering down below; only a confused babble of voices and then a great shuffling of feet.

But Marcus was smiling now. He said to Gerd, "That was a true Roman speaking. They never surrender. They may withdraw to another place, but they never surrender. They will destroy the Iceni, do not fear."

Gerd said to herself so as not to trouble him, "Aye, and they will leave the people to fend for themselves and be butchered and tortured. That is Rome, aye, that is Rome."

Marcus did not hear her. He was fast asleep in the straw, breathing easily and smiling, as though all was well in his mind now.

Dawn was coming across the broad river and striking into the cold room when Gerd shook him and woke him. Her face was pale and serious and her hair was tangled all over her shoulders. "I did not wake you before," she said, "but now I must, if you are to live. The army has gone. The city is almost deserted. All those who can walk have followed the general out of the gates. Only the old and maimed are left to face the burners. I do not intend to burn with them."

Marcus shook his head to clear it and said, "I do not think that I could march far. I will try to get a weapon from somewhere, an old sword or an axe, and I will get you to tie me against the gates so that I do not fall down. Then I may be able to strike a blow or two for Rome. I may be able to avenge Tigidius, if Mithras will only smile on me, before the Iceni get to me."

But Gerd slapped him quite hard across the face. "You talk like a fool," she said. "Now get up and lean on me. I have not looked after you so long to let you throw your life away uselessly. Come, come, you silly child, I have arranged with an old man I know to take us on his mule-cart out of this place. He won't wait for ever. Come now.

He began to push her away, but she was too strong for him and made him get to his feet. She even pinned his cloak about his head and shoulders to keep the chill morning air from him. And then she helped him down the creaking stairs.

A white-haired old man dressed in greasy hides sat on a cart outside, bobbing up and down with terror. "Hurry, hurry," he croaked! "I have just heard that the tribes have pushed into the town lower down the river. Get on the cart now, or I must leave you. Hurry, or we shall be dead. If I were not a good man, I should not wait."

Gerd helped Marcus up among the piles of hide and the sticks of furniture that the old man was trying to save. She said in a cold voice, "You save us not because you are a good man, for in truth you are one of the biggest rascals in Londinium, Gyrth. You save us because you know that if you did not, my cousin Brand would come looking for you one day, and he would ask a question or two before he knocked you on the head with his axe."

Gyrth whipped the tired mule along the street and shouted back, "That red-handed pirate! That sea wolf! I am sorry down to the cellars of my heart that I ever promised him to look after you. See where it has got me! I could have been away safely an hour ago, if I had not waited for this lazy dog of a Roman at your bidding."

They went along narrow lanes; not down the wide roads. Only a few old folk sat at their doorways waiting, as though they had given up all hope and did not wish to be saved.

Gerd said sternly, "My cousin Brand set you up in trade here, didn't he? He brought you over from Frisia in his ship, didn't he? Well, man, show some gratitude and stop bleating like an old sheep."

They turned northward after they had gone for an hour along the river, and soon ran into lanes where the hawthorns and alders grew thickly, and hid them from view.

Then Marcus raised himself and looked back. In a dull voice he said, "Smoke is rising from the city. It is a

138

doomed place now. They will leave nothing of it standing, and no folk alive."

Gerd was trying to comb her hair as they jolted along the rutted lane. "Yes," she said, "and you thought you could save that old midden heap! The more fool you! It was not worth saving. Now lie back and try to get some rest. I will wake you if you need to be woken."

23

The Midland Forest

BUT SHE did not wake him through that day. She did not think that he needed to see the burned villages, or the smoking waste of Verulam. He slept deeply with exhaustion, though the groaning old cart bumped cruelly across fields and through watersplashes. Once she turned back his shirt and looked at his shoulder wound. It was still red and angry-looking, but was healing well now; and the bruise on his chest had changed from blue to a yellowish color. She said, "Ula Buriash knows his business. He should have been a doctor. That should have been his trade."

Old Gyrth looked back and said, grumbling, "I wish we had him here now, he could give me something for my aching back. I have not gone so far and so fast for many years. I shall never walk upright again and after all this jolting."

Gerd clambered over the load in the cart and almost

threw the old man aside. "Give me the reins and the whip," she said. "A man is too old to live when he gets too old to drive a cart. I must tell my cousin Brand what a fine fellow he set up in business."

Gyrth put his hands together and said, "I beg you, Gerd, do not be so hasty. I am not complaining. I was only putting forward a point of view. A man has the right to do that, hasn't he? You would not deny him that, would you? Saxons believe in free speaking, don't they?"

Gerd drove the cart up a grassy slope, to be away from the lane now. She said, "Oh, go to sleep, and let me get on with what must be done. I like your silence better than your speaking."

It was late afternoon before they halted. By then, even Gerd could see that the mule would fall in its tracks if they did not rest. Now they had come out of the farmland, and away from all roads and lanes. They were at the edge of the great forest that stretched on northward almost to Lindum and the Abus. So she drew in under the oak boughs and awoke Marcus.

"We shall rest awhile," she said. "The mule will graze and we will go into the wood and see if we can find something to eat. There might be a young deer we could run down, or a stupid hare that will sit still while we throw a stone at him."

Old Gyrth nodded. He said, "While you are away, I will make a little wood fire inside the glade here so that no one will see the smoke. Keep your eyes open for berries or wild apples. At least they will be better than nothing if you do not find some meat to cook."

Gerd turned on him sharply and said, "You get on with your fire and keep your advice to yourself, old sheep. And if anyone comes, get behind a bush. Don't run out to greet them and tell them about your bad back. If they are Iceni they might give you an even worse one."

The forest was very still. Soon the trees were so thickly grown that it was quite dark among them. But from time to time they came upon little clearings where pools stood, or streams trickled, and the grass was a deep green unlike the dusty brown hay of the fields. They sat down to rest in such a glade, with the amber rays of the sun striking in shafts over their shoulders and turning all the leaves and boughs to a deep, golden color.

They drank from the water and nibbled a handful of berries. And while they sat there, a young hare came from a clump of ferns and sat up to look at them more closely. Marcus said, "Well, now is our chance. I think I might have him down from this range."

But Gerd put her hand on his arm and shook her head. "I have a mind to let this one go," she said smiling. "We may be hungry, but it seems a shame to rob this one of his life. He has not had it long. I think we owe it to him to spare him, as the gods have spared us."

Marcus clucked his tongue and the young hare heard it and shambled away on legs that seemed too long for his body. He said, "I always thought that you Saxons were a wild savage folk, yet you shrink back from hurting the little beast."

Gerd began to wash her hands and face in the water and to look down at her reflection to see that her hair was tidy. She said, "What you Romans think of us hardly matters. Romans do not understand us because we like to live privately in the forests and not in crowded cities. We prefer to be among trees and not in musty old houses. Besides, I liked that little hare. I liked the way it twitched its nose. Why should I kill it because I am hungry? There is no more to say. Eat your berries and we will go back to the old man. The mule will be rested by now. We must see that the fire is stamped out and the ashes scattered among the bushes, or someone may follow our trail."

But when they got back to the edge of the wood there was no fire to stamp out, and no mule either. They followed the tracks of the wheels for a while in the grass and then lost them when the ground got harder.

Gerd looked up at Marcus with a wry smile. "The old sheep has left us," she said. "He has gone on alone to save his tattered old fleece somewhere else. Well, at least he got us safely out of the city for which we should be thankful."

Marcus said, "Yes, it is something."

He stood silently for a while with the setting sun at his left hand, then pointing before him toward the forest he said, "The north lies in the direction I point. If we go that way through the trees we must sooner or later strike the Watling Street that runs across country."

Gerd said, "Why do you wish to get back onto a road, having been at such pains to get off one? Are you Romans so much in love with roads that you cannot bear to be out of sight of one?"

Marcus smiled at her. "I do not like roads any more than you do," he said. "I have marched along too many of them in my time. But somewhere along that road the fourteenth and twentieth legions will come marching, ten thousand of them and more. And where they are, we shall be safe. Our troubles will be over."

Gerd plucked a grass stalk and began to chew it. She said, "You may be safe with them, but they will take me for British and I do not think that they will be any kinder to me than the Iceni would have been. A Roman spear is just as sharp to me as any other sort."

Marcus took her by the hand and said, "I shall tell them who you are and what you have done for me. They will listen to the son of Ostorius the tribune."

But now Gerd pulled away from him, her face set, and said, "Perhaps it is right for you to go back to your people. But they are not my people. The best they would do would be to set me working in their camp kitchens and treat me like a slave. My folk are freeborn and not slaves. I could not bear that. I should hang myself with shame—then all this wandering would have been a waste. I might as well have stayed in the city and let the Iceni hang me."

Marcus felt his chest and shoulder aching again and grew impatient. "Look, girl," he said, "you are talking about people you do not know. Many of the twentieth look like you, sound like you, and even think like you. Some of them may even know your cousin Brand."

She smiled at this. "They will say little that is good about him," she said. "He has never gone out of his way to make them like him. But I think he would like you. I think that you are his sort of man. Look, Marcus, why do we not go to the south and find our way to Vectis? We could take ship with him. We could persuade him to go anywhere you wished, provided he could find good pickings. He would do it, I promise you. He would do anything for me. He would sail as far as Alexandria if I asked him."

Marcus gazed at her strangely then. "Alexandria," he said. "Do you know, I have a sister there. I would love to see her again, and joggle her baby on my knee. I have not seen my sister for most of my life."

Then suddenly he came out of his dream and said, "But she would not know me now. She has other things to concern her. No, we will do as I say. My duty is to the legions. We will go north. And I swear to you on my honor that you shall be well treated. Come now, before the light goes altogether."

So Gerd sighed, and then shook her head. But when she saw that he was determined to make his way through the forest she followed him, and before long they were back among the dark trees.

They were able to walk for an hour before the light went at last, and the strange darkness of the midland forest came down on them. Marcus began to stumble over roots and bang himself against tree trunks. Gerd had always lived in forests, and seemed to sense the overhanging boughs and the sudden hollows even before she came to them. She took the Roman's hand and guided him for a time. Then at last she stopped and said in a whisper, "This is as much as we should do."

143

He said, "No, we must press forward, girl. I still have strength enough to continue, if you will lead me. We still have some distance to cover."

But she held him back. "This is where we stay tonight," she said firmly. "If we go on, we shall never arrive anywhere. Look behind you."

Marcus turned, and along the way they had come he sensed the rustle of stealthy movements. He even thought he saw dark shapes flitting from bush to bush.

He said, "What is it, Gerd?"

She grimly, "If you wait a little, you will see their eyes, and then you will not need to ask. I thought I scented them half a mile back, but now I know."

Then Marcus saw the glint of amber eyes, at waist level all around him among the undergrowth. "They are wolves," he said. "I did not know that there were wolves here. But how silent they are!"

Gerd said, "Aye, they are silent enough when they are tracking, but they will howl shortly when they begin their rush. Come on, into this oak tree with you. They are not the best climbers in the world, these wolves. There are some things we can do better than they can."

Now he did not argue with the girl, but clambered up, as she told him, drawing her beside him. As they stood on the first stout branch, there was a sudden fierce rush below, then a dark shape flung itself up toward them. Marcus felt something brush against his foot, heard the snapping of jaws, and then the thud as the wolf fell down onto the turf.

"That was too close," he said, "we must climb higher, friend."

In the darkness Gerd said, "Aye, some of them are good leapers, but that one did not know his trade too well. An old dog-wolf would have had you down by now, but that was only a youth at the business."

Marcus shuddered suddenly. Then he heard a rustling beside him and at last Gerd said, "I have taken off my shift so to climb as a rope. Now hold the end of it and I will go up first and draw you afterward. I have yet to meet the oak tree I could not climb. Come now, the pack is gathering."

Marcus began to protest, but the Saxon said, "Save your breath for climbing, man. We are in the dark. I shall put it on again when we are safe. Move your legs while you still have legs to move."

And when they were high up in the thick-leaved tree, he gazed down again. It seemed that a thousand glowing sparks were twinkling below him on the forest floor.

Then Gerd said, "That is what I call a legion—though what its number is I do not know or care. Here we are safe in this fork of the tree. We can lean back and wait till the daylight sends the pack slinking away. Let me bind your belt round the bough so that you do not slip off, in the night."

He felt her strong hands fastening him safely. Then he said, "By Mithras and all his Lights, I do not know what I would have done without you. I wish that Tigidius could have met you, Gerd, he would have fallen in love with such a woman."

In the darkness Gerd sighed impatiently. "Perhaps," she said, "but he would have been too late. Now go to sleep, if you can. There may be much to do tomorrow."

24

Strange Feasting

For a long time Marcus could not sleep. Boughs creaked all about him and the night was heavy with the rustling of leaves and the cries of hunting animals below. Once a great bird flapped close to him, then veered away on rattling wings, shrieking out a warning to the other birds.

Then in spite of the chilly breeze that shook the bough that supported him, and in spite of all the unknown sounds that filled his ears, he fell back against the fork of the tree into a dream in which he and Tigidius were running along that road again, out of Camulodunum. He saw the overgrown shrine set above the sunken lane and smelled the sacrificial meat burning on the altar fire. And in the dream, he went with the centurion to the hut, and there found a table laden with good food. There were walnuts, plums in syrup, oysters, honey cakes, dates and golden figs, set in silver dishes. On wooden trenchers lay meats of all kinds; and the whitest crispest bread he had ever seen. In the dream Tigidius said to him, "I told you there would be something to eat here, tribune. But you, with your thoughts of death, would not believe me. Now do you trust my word?"

Marcus nodded and slapped the centurion on the shoulder. They sat at the table and began to eat. The food was quite the finest they had ever tasted. Tigidius said, "If only your father were here now, boy!" And just then

146

Marcus looked up; and there, at the head of the table sat Ostorius, looking just as he ever was, his face brown and wrinkled, his eyes gleaming and his mouth smiling. He said as he nibbled at a chicken leg, "Well, Marcus, this is the life, hey? When old comrades gather together for the feast, hey? That is the life!" Then he began to tell a long story about a feast he had once attended as a young soldier outside Damascus. He described all the colored fruits and the syrups and the wine served with cream upon it from golden cups. As he was in the middle of his story another voice spoke out of the darkness behind the smoking altar and said, "Rome is eating up the world. The world is Rome's delicacy. All goes into Rome's stomach and there is nothing left for the other folk."

Marcus glanced around in annoyance that his father should be interrupted so. And standing behind the altar he saw a woman dressed in a grey robe, with a hood that mostly covered her face. But he knew who it was. He said to her, "If you have come for your brooch, you can have it, and welcome. Only, let us get on with our feasting. I have not seen my father and my old comrade for long enough."

The woman shook her head and said, "I have come for something else and it is not my brooch."

In her right hand she held a stick that was a snake. Sometimes it wriggled and then it became stiff and straight. Marcus watched it with a plum in his mouth. He could taste the syrup quite clearly. He swallowed it and said, "I have never seen such a stick before. Is it from Egypt, woman? I hear they have such sticks there."

But she did not answer him. Instead, she leaned across the altar, right through the flames of the fire, and struck upon the table where the feasters sat. Then Marcus saw that the feast had gone, and in its place lay a dead sheep with its wool charred and its yellow teeth showing between its grinning lips. The woman smiled and said, "Take, eat, Romans. This is your feasting now."

147

Marcus turned round in fury to see what his father would think of such a thing; but his father had vanished, and so had Tigidius, and now he sat alone at the moss-covered board.

He looked again at the dead sheep and then saw that that it wore his medallion about its burned neck, the one he had given to Aranrhod. Now the medallion was dull and scratched and not brightly-polished as he had always kept it. He said in anger, "There will be a price to pay for this. The legions will gather when they hear how my father has been dishonored. Aye, they will gather, woman."

She laughed at his words and stretched out her snake-stick toward him. At first he stood there, but then the flicking tongue came so close to his face that he drew back his head and struck at it.

He was still doing this when he saw that the snake was a green oak twig and that the woman who held it was Gerd. She was touching his face with it gently to waken him, and putting her finger to her lips to warn him not to cry out.

He saw the billowing waves of the treetops all about as far as the eye could reach, and above them, the blue sky and the white clouds. Gerd whispered, "Do not speak, Marcus, Look below us, but not not speak."

Marcus looked down through the thick foliage. He saw that their oak tree was placed on the lip of a deep gully, and that now this gully was crowded with men. From their leather helmets and cuirasses he knew that they were auxiliaries of the legions. Many of them wore their fair hair long, onto the shoulders, and he guessed that they were a German contingent.

Then he turned in the fork of the tree and gazed in the other direction; men were there too, men with dark hair cropped short, squatting on the ground, their long javelins prodding upwards. These were Macedonians.

148

Gerd edged slowly along the bough and whispered, "They have been coming in for two hours, since before dawn. The wolves heard them and fled. These are fiercer wolves. We cannot go down now. They would spear us before we could say who we were."

Marcus nodded. "I did not expect this," he said. "If they had been men of the legions proper, I could have gone to their tribunes; but you are right, they would never let us set foot on the ground. The forest is alive with them. There must be thousands. They have gathered for a strange feasting. It is like a dream."

25

Crab's Claws

As the morning passed, Marcus made a small space among the leaves so that he could see before him. And then he said, "The fourteenth and the twentieth are set out ahead. I can recognise their eagles."

Cohort after cohort waited, formed into squares, lounging on their spears. At either side of them sat cavalrymen with their long swords across their thighs.

Marcus said, half in pride, half in fear now, "Mithras, but they have come, the legions. They have come with a vengeance!"

Gerd whispered, "It is a fearsome thing to belong to such a people. You are so many and so unforgiving."

Marcus said suddenly, "I had thought to have cheered

when I saw my own folk again, but now I am almost afraid of them myself. These men have come from destroying Mona; they have marched across the land from one side to the other without resting. Someone will have to pay a high price for that marching. Look down at their faces. They are of iron, like their swords, these men."

Then quite clearly in the morning air they heard a voice calling out through a trumpet to the assembled armies. Marcus said, "It is the general. It is old Death Bringer himself. This must be the last battle of the world."

The thin clear voice sounded through the forest, echoing off the trees, sending the creatures to their holes and lairs. "Romans," it said, "you stand in the cold morning winds now, but soon you will be warm. The riders have brought news that they are coming, the Iceni and their hangers-on. You will not have long to wait."

For a while there was some chattering among the auxiliaries below, but as the general's voice grew more savage, even they fell silent. He spoke the words they had waited to hear.

"Brothers, for we of Rome are all brothers, you have seen what they do, these British. Many of you have lost comrades and kinsmen. Today, unless you stand fast, you will lose your own lives. Since you are men, not children, and wish to know the truth, I will tell you the truth. It is your right to know it. These British mean to frighten you out of this province. They mean to send you scurrying like hares to the sea. They mean to make your name stink through the world as cowards. They mean to drag down the very walls of Rome. Of course, you will let them do that. Of course, you will let them do to you what they have done to your kinsmen and comrades. Of course you will. That is what Romans like, is it not, to be captured and spiked on sharp stakes? To be flung into vats of boiling water and watch their flesh melting? To be turned slowly on spits over charcoal fires? We like that, don't we, lads? We thrive on it, don't we?"

150

As he said this, a great roar burst from the forest. It was as though the trees were shaken by an earthquake.

Suetonius went on, "Aye, we like it, I can tell. But we like it better when *we* are the victors. We like it better when *we* see the enemy turn and fling down their weapons and run screaming from us. And that is what they will do today, I promise you. I swear to almighty Jupiter, and on the bones of all my ancestors, the enemy will run today. I give you my solemn word—and I will fall on my sword here and now before you if you doubt it—that today you will wipe them out as though they had never been. Do you believe me, old friends? Do you believe Suetonius?"

Once again the trees rocked and the birds flew up crying into the air. Leaves fell to the earth in a green shower.

Then the great voice lost its passion and spoke sharply. "Very well then, my legions, remember your drill. Stand in close order, shield grating on shield. Throw your javelins true when your centurions give the word. Do not be put off your cast by blue-painted faces. Any fool can paint his face, but not any fool can cast a javelin. Go forth in line with your swords when your officers give the advance. Poke at their blue faces, my brothers; that will make them skip. And when the horns blow, stand still. Do not move, or then the cavalry on either flank will take over from you to give you a breather. My fine cavalry will close on them like the claws of a crab, nipping them as they run. Ah, you will see, my brothers, you will see the pincers nipping hard."

Again the earth shuddered with the stamping and spear-thudding and shield-beating.

The voice broke through again in its last command: "One word of warning. Your work today is to trap them and kill them; that is your task and no other. Do not think of plunder. Do not turn your minds to gold and pretty weapons. Every second that you pause to pick up such rubbish will kill a comrade for you, and could kill you too. Do as I say, and by this day's end, my brothers, you shall have all the plunder you can carry. You shall be so rich that Nero himself will envy you. Old Stomach himself will envy you!"

As he finished the legions howled again. High in the oak tree, Gerd closed her eyes and whispered, "I am afraid. Even to be near a Roman like you, I am afraid."

Marcus bowed his head and said quietly, "I cannot believe that once my father spoke such words to his men. He was such a kind man. I cannot believe it."

But Gerd had stopped listening. Pointing toward the little space in the leaves, she said, "Look, they are coming. Boadicea's folk are coming, and she is leading them."

26

Kinsman of Caratacus

ACROSS the shaggy moorland that lay at the beginning of the gully moved a great horde. Far into the distance the earth was black with them. Some were walking, some dancing, some riding gaily on unbroken ponies. Great wagons decorated with colored banners and white skulls set on poles moved among them. Above them and behind them black ravens wheeled, hungry for the feasting. Hounds ran here and there, noses to the ground, seeking the prey they had been promised; women strummed on lyres or blew down bone flutes; children ran in companies waving bright flags and laughing at the holiday.

From place to place chariots raced with gaunt chieftains in them, shepherding the tribes, giving messages and orders. One chieftain from the far west rode on a bull, painted green to represent the old god Poseidon, and carrying a trident in his hand. His headdress was not of bronze but of seaweed. He tottered helplessly for a while and then fell to the ground among his laughing folk. He was laughing too.

Marcus said, "They do not need soldiers to kill them. They will kill themselves. Look, they are drawing the wagons across the mouth of the gully so that the Romans shall not escape. Before this day is out, they may regret they have shut the gate against themselves."

But Gerd said sadly, "They outnumber the legions, ten to one. They have only to come forward as they are doing now to smother the men below us."

And for a moment it seemed that the auxiliaries had thought of that, for their excited chattering had stopped and many of them were looking over their shoulders to see where they could run, if the worst came to the worst.

Then the Celtic battle-horde halted. Boadicea, her face painted white, her hair flying loose in the wind, stood up in her black wagon in the front rank. And that wind blew her words into the ears of the waiting Romans. "My children," she called, "this will not take us long, then we can dance and sing at our leisure. Today you face creatures—I will not call them men—who bathe in warm water, eat dainty food, sleep on feather beds, and scent themselves with myrrh. Creatures who have a fat old lute-player for their king. Creatures who think so much of their stomachs that they eat the oyster but throw away the pearl that is in the shell."

Marcus did not hear what else she said, because he suddenly felt so hungry that he almost fell from the oak tree.

Then all at once he knew that she had stopped speaking, and saw that the tribes could wait no longer, but were running forward in a thick mass toward the legions.

Then he heard the hard-voiced decurions below going at their trade. "First rank, cast—kneel. Second rank, cast—

153

kneel. Third rank, cast—kneel. Wait for it. Wait for it. Now, swords out! Forward!"

Everywhere this was being said, and always in the same voice, as though one man had said it all.

And then the rushing Britons were down, men and horses and chariots. Some turned and fled, horses riderless, chariots banging about without drivers, all in confusion.

And through the confused air came the sound of the silver trumpets. The legions standing dead still. . . . The riders coming out on either side from the woods, slashing down at everything moving. . . . Then the trumpets again and the cavalry wheeling and going back under cover, as though they were rehearsing maneuvres on Mars' Field in Rome.

And now the general once again: "Nicely nipped, my crabs. Oh, nicely nipped. But see if you can get more next time, boys. Just a few hundred more and I'll be satisfied."

The Iceni did not seem as though they believed what had happened to them, for they came again almost immediately. And once more the decurions chanted, once more the horse came out. Once more Suetonius spoke down the trumpet, always asking for more, for more. He was like a hungry god.

It was midday now and the sun stood overhead. Gerd said, "Surely they must stop and go away. It *must* be over."

But Marcus did not answer. He knew that it would not be over until Suetonius stopped calling down the horn—and that would mean there were no more to kill, that his hunger was satisfied at last.

Then in the middle afternoon, when the flies were swarming in the oak tree, a thing happened that held both armies silent. Down the trampled field toward the legions came a white-haired old chieftain sitting bolt-upright on a dappled pony. His long moustaches reached down to his breast in the Gallic style. The burnished bronze he wore belonged to a past generation. The gold about his neck and wrists glittered for a quarter of a mile. Before him on the red Spanish saddle sat a small boy no older than four, and wearing the same bronze and the same tartan cloak.

Marcus squinted at the man and said, "He is of the royal house of the Catuvellauni, some kinsman of Caratacus. I did not think we had left any of them alive. He must have come from far away, from across the sea, perhaps."

Behind the dappled pony rode seven youths, on good horses, naked to the waist and shaking lances. All had the same look of the old man in front of them. Only the red bars of paint across their faces and bodies were different.

Gerd looked at them and said, "Woden, Woden! Not one but would be a king in my land. I pray for them."

Suetonius let them come within a hundred paces before he called to the archers. And then the youths fell one by one. The youngest of them was dragged by his leather thongs almost to spear-thrust of the first ranks of the legions.

But still the old man rode on, never once looking back at the youths. And when he was up to the first stockade of pointing javelins, he cried out in perfect Latin, "Where is the Butcher? Let him come down and face me."

For an instant, Roman heads turned to see if Suetonius would take the challenge. But no answer came, and then the spearmen began to thrust at the old man. Angrily he slashed out with his long sword and five men went down under him. Then a Balearic slinger stepped forward and taking aim, knocked the chieftain off his saddle with the first stone. The spearmen shrugged their shoulders, then pinned him as he tried to rise.

By some strange chance the dappled horse broke free and turned back toward the wagons, with the little boy clinging to its mane unharmed.

Marcus said hoarsely, "They will let him go back. They

are not monsters. It is their one salvation. They give honor where it is due."

Just as he finished, the trumpets screamed again and from either side the whole cavalry came forward, as though they were called on to wipe out a whole contingent.

But when they reached the little boy on the dappled horse they reined in, making a guard of honor through which he must pass. He did not seem to notice them, but rode on, looking toward Boadicea.

Then, almost wearily, the captain of horse nodded to his squadron and they closed the funnel. They used their swords so reluctantly that it seemed as though they carried lead in their hands, not thin steel.

Afterward they led the dappled horse back to Suetonius with silent mockery against their general.

Marcus leaned his head against the bough and wept. He was not the only Roman who wept that day.

Then the whole army moved, as though this had been the final signal for the destruction. And as the sun sank, the Britons, penned in by their own wagons, fell in great heaps upon the moorland. Families died together there; the children still playing with their garlands, the women still holding their babies, or with the flute at their lips.

And when dusk began to fall, Gerd said, "I have been sick, Marcus, I could not help it. I feel ill now and must get down this tree."

He nodded. "I am the same, sister," he said. "I feel that I shall always be sick now."

There was no one to hinder them below. The legions were spread far and wide, gathering what they had been promised.

27

Old Friend and Enemy

AND when they were on the ground again Marcus said, "Before we leave this terrible place, there is someone I must look for."

Hand in hand they went over the moorland, past the piled slain and the dead horses and mutilated oxen. And at last they came to the black wagon that had been the queen's. It lay keeled over, its wheels broken on one side. She still lay in it among her women.

Marcus looked down at the painted face and the ash-covered hair that had once been as tawny as a fox. And while he was looking at her, Boadicea's dark-lidded eyes opened wide and fixed on him. Then quite clearly she said, "You have come to see me at the last, old friend and enemy. If you have brought my brooch back, then you can save yourself the trouble. I do not need it now, and the pillagers would steal it in any case. It is yours. Keep it forever and remember me."

He fell on his knees before her and bowed his head, as though she were his mother. She smiled once before her eyes closed. "I shall not forget you, lady," he said. He could not find the words to say any more.

Gerd touched him on the shoulder and said, "She will not wake again. See the froth at her lips. She is poisoned. Come away, the soldiers are sweeping round this way."

Marcus let her lead him until they came to an overturned chariot behind the wagon. And there he halted.

"That is the banner of the Coritani," he said. "Cynwas should be here."

The prince lay on the floor of the broken war-cart, three arrows in him, his arms still clasped about Aranrhod, whose hair had been brushed till it looked like silk. Her mouth was open, as though she had been chattering to her brother when all the breath went from her.

Gerd said, "She is wearing a gold medallion, Marcus. They must have robbed a Roman before they died."

Marcus shook his head. "A Roman would be proud to give his medallion to such a child," he said, and turned away into the dusk.

In all the movements to and fro of the plunderers, the two were not noticed, and so they came from the battle-field and down into a misty hollow by nightfall.

Marcus said wearily, "Now I have seen enough of war. There is no place in the ninth legion for such as I am now. I have lost all heart for killing. I can find sheepskin to write on. I shall send in my resignation to Petillius in Lindum. I will do it correctly, giving my reasons, and will not just skulk away like a common deserter."

Gerd nodded. Then she smiled and said, "The Romans have no further need of you, I think. From what I saw today, they will be here to the end of the world without your help. But I shall not stay in this land, for I can see that the Roman vengeance will be terrible. It will show no mercy to anyone. I shall make my way down to Vectis and go aboard my cousin Brand's ship. If you are wise, you will come with me and sail to see your sister in Alexandria."

Marcus passed his hand over his face. "Brand would not want a weakling like me," he said. "Besides, I have no passage-money for him."

Then Gerd held out something that glistened in the moonlight. "That is arranged," she said smiling. "I have that golden medallion we saw. It is of Roman craftsman-ship and should be worth something."

At first Marcus almost struck her in his grief. But then

he calmed down again. She had helped him so much. Besides, if she had not taken it, someone else would have; someone less worthy.

He nodded slowly and said, "Yes, Saxon, we will go to Vectis. Where else is there to go?"

The Author

HENRY TREECE was a poet, novelist, critic, playwright, and historian. The Queen's Brooch was the last novel he wrote for young people before his tragic death.

His special interests were Celtic history and the Vikings. He was best known for his brilliant novels for adults and children about the Dark Ages.